# LOOKING FOR TROUBLE



## AND OTHER MOSTLY YEOVILLE STORIES

# LOOKING FOR TROUBLE

AND OTHER MOSTLY YEOVILLE STORIES

COLLEEN HIGGS

First published in March 2012 by Hands-On Books
PO Box 385, Athlone, 7760, South Africa
http://modjaji.book.co.za
modjaji.books@gmail.com

ISBN 978-1-920397-42-5

Editor: Karen Jennings
Cover artwork: Jesse Breytenbach and Life is Awesome
Book and cover design: Natascha Mostert and Life is Awesome
Author photograph: Liesl Jobson

Printed and bound by Mega Digital, Cape Town
Set in Garamond

DISCLAIMER: All characters appearing in this work are fictitious. Any resemblance to real persons, living or dead, is purely coincidental.

for Graeme and Graeme and Belinda and
Caroline and Lili and to everyone who has ever
lived in Yeoville and loved it

# About Yeoville

These stories are set in Yeoville in the late eighties, early nineties. Many people of my generation struggled to take their lives seriously in a country that in the eighties seemed to be hurtling towards a civil war or general meltdown. The speed of the transition to democracy in the early nineties was enlivening. The stories show what life was like in a particular place in South Africa at a time in which everything was about to change.

Yeoville, like Ithaca, was and is a state of mind as much as a place. It was a grey area in all kinds of ways. People came from the Northern suburbs and from as far afield as Kempton Park and Alberton to experience Yeoville. It was trendy, vibey, stylish, down at heel, grungy, cosmopolitan, cutting edge, diverse, full of animated, heated talk, a hot-bed of dissent, debate, surveillance, fear, violence, sex, drugs and alcohol. Most nights of the week you could listen to live music, smoke, drink, flirt, dance, and eat at any one of a number of eateries, Ba Pita, Tandoori Chicken, Elaine's, The Black Sun, Mama's Pizzas, Scandalo's, Times Square, the Train, Midnight Express. Those who lived there at the time had a sense that it was a special place to live, and that it was a particular time that was already changing, but they didn't know exactly how fast.

In Yeoville everyone you ever slept with would have slept with at least one other person you knew really well. Or be close friends with someone you knew well or worked with. It was an incestuous village. The people who lived there were film-makers, musos – like James Phillips – journalists, film-makers, out lesbians, trade union leaders, students, lecturers, writers, Jewish pensioners, podiatrists, and bank clerks. A Beat poet, theatre directors (Barney Simon), actors, human rights lawyers, taxi drivers, teachers – some who worked in suburban schools and others in Soweto – librarians, Marxists, 'Trots', Catholic revolutionaries, sangomas, dopers, stoners, architects, social critics, photographers, Black Sash advice office workers, literacy teachers, playwrights, people who worked in the movies in props and costumes, whose houses and flats looked like sets. People belonged to the ANC, the UDF, Inkatha, women's groups, veggie co-ops, feminist reading groups, the Yeovillle Residents' Association. If you weren't a traditional omnivore, you ate vegan, vegetarian, macrobiotic, dairy free, wheat free, no red meat. Many people were in therapy at least once a week.

When I lived in Yeoville from the mid eighties to the mid nineties the layers of living there in the past were present to me. I lived in Yeoville as an infant in the early sixties, as a teenager in the mid seventies and then finally as a young during the late eighties and early nineties. As an infant, my family lived at the top of the hill in Bellevue East. My mother would walk down the hill to buy groceries most days, pushing a pram. In summer we often spent part of the morning in the paddle pool in the park. I was a teenager when my family moved back to Joburg; we lived in a flat at the top of Cavendish Road. I used to walk down the hill to the library and to the public swimming pool. In his late thirties my father had to stop playing polo in Lesotho (my parents work permits were refused) and had to start catching buses into town, from Yeoville. He caught the Number 19 bus into town to the corner of Jeppe and Rissik. He carried a briefcase with a combination lock and was trying to earn enough to support a family of six. No more polo, no more galloping on well trained horses across dusty fields. He became a sales rep for Pfizer's veterinary/agriculture division. On Saturday afternoons I would catch the number 19 to von Weilligh Square and then walk to the Carlton Skyrink to ice skate and hang out.

When people talked about Yeoville, they usually meant Bellevue East, Upper Houghton, and Berea as well. The neighbourhoods that bordered Yeoville were also called Yeoville. The famous Rockey Street was officially Raleigh Street in Yeoville proper, but no-one called it Raleigh Street.

Yeoville is situated on a ridge, on one of the rande that make up the Witwatersrand. At the top of Yeoville is the water tower and from the flats high up you get a wonderful view of the city and of the suburbs, all under the high blue Highveld sky.

# Contents

# Spying

I bumped into your folks at the Hypermarket the other day. I hadn't thought much about you in years. They were buying a ladder and a new washing machine. It was such a shock to see them after all this time. They still look exactly the same, just older. Where does your old lady buy her dresses? I have never seen dresses like that except at a shop in Parkhurst in the 70s. Geraldine Gowns. She said you're still in London, got a kid now and all. Seeing them like that set me thinking about you and about us.

Do you remember the time I spied on you? You knew I was there, but not till you got to the parking lot. You recognized my old Toyota bakkie. You were furious and I can't say I blame you. I'm surprised Diane didn't notice the bakkie too. Perhaps she did, but she didn't say anything. You'd have mentioned that when we spoke on the phone later and you gave me hell. Even months after we split up you still told me all kinds of stuff about her that you shouldn't have, like how she was on the pill. Later on I realized that the word stalking applied to me. Not that I made a big habit of it or anything. The two of you had been to a movie, at Rosebank. I saw you riding up the escalator holding hands. You a bit taller than her, your straight dark hair a stark contrast to her long wavy blonde hair, your face relaxed, looking down at her as she spoke. She was wearing a loose cotton dress in two shades of lime green, and slip slops. I was sitting at that coffee shop at the top of the escalators drinking rooibos tea, my heart beating too fast already for coffee. She looked like a school girl version of a Botticelli Venus.

I'd worked it all out, we had been talking about movies, and you told me that you were planning to see a movie at the French film festival, *Monsieur Hire*. I asked you to come with me for a walk, just to Delta Park or Emmarentia, round the lakes. I was sitting in my flat battling with that caged-in feeling I sometimes used to get on weekends in Yeoville, when I didn't have plans. You said you couldn't, you were busy. That's how I knew you'd be there.

After you two strolled down the passage to the parking garage, I took my time, finished my tea, waited so you'd be in your car, then I followed you in my bakkie, just a bit of the way down Jan Smuts. It was dark, but my bakkie was pretty distinctive and I just didn't have the balls for it, so to speak. You were going back to her folks' place in Ferndale. I knew the address from looking it up in the phone book. I thought about how the two of you were each staying with your own folks and not together, even though you lived together in Cape Town. Your folks were especially heavy about sex, even though mine had the Christian thing, it was a thin, recently acquired veneer and they were much cooler about things like that. Their philosophy was, "It's your life." They probably didn't get as involved because they had lots of their own hassles, with money and other stuff. My brothers were in the army. The thing with your old lady was that she couldn't deal with the thought of you having sex. I never figured out if it was because she was jealous or because the whole idea of sex was just too much for her. Probably both. Your old man must have slipped it to her at least the once.

Why was I surprised that you got tied up with Diane before things were over between us? I know a lot of the messiness was my fault. I wasn't exactly faithful while you were at varsity in Cape Town. But you'd left me behind. Ag, your fault, my fault, never mind who's fault. We broke up and you found a new chick straight away. Even before we broke up. She was part of the reason we broke up. Just like with you and the chick you were involved with before me too, Susie, was it? Only I didn't think it applied to us in the beginning, because it was true love, what we had. That's what you said, well not in those words, because you've got a way with words that made me want to believe you.

The other weird thing about that time was that if you hadn't been going to see a movie with her, you might well have gone walking with me, or we might have gone to a movie. We used to go for walks, I would cry and beg you to come back to me. You would look uncomfortable, but you wouldn't agree to come back. You wouldn't say anything. You'd wait a bit then change the subject. You would even fetch me from the airport when you moved to Cape Town, and I visited there. We would go for drinks somewhere, the Lord Milner hotel. You knew all these cool places where you could have a drink. The Holiday Inn in Gardens the one time, and there was that short TV star from Dallas, Miss Ellie's granddaughter, the one with the long blonde hair. Was her name Charlene or Charmaine? Something like that. Only we didn't know she was coming, just that there was this hectic buzz at the Gardens Holiday Inn, and snacks all put out and it was hard to buy a drink, but you managed. And then we left before she arrived, but it was cool to be there and to feel the excitement and to be too cool to stay and try to rub shoulders with an American TV star. We ate a few of the peanuts and things that were meant to be there for her real fans.

After that you took me back to the place I was staying at in Oranjezicht with an old school friend, Clara, the one who'd married a rich guy, a plastic surgeon. They had gone to bed already, you came into my bedroom and kissed me, and pulled my shirt up, and kissed my breasts. And then you went home to her. And that's why I kept thinking that maybe you'd come back to me someday. Only you haven't and you won't and by now I don't even want you to. And I have moved on, even though it may not seem like it, what with me coming out with all this old shit. But sometimes I get nostalgic, not for you, but for those days, because that was when I was young, and so were you and you knew me, like in those before and after pictures, sometimes it feels like you are the only one who knew the before picture of me, when I was still so serious and innocent. And sometimes I wonder if Diane ever questioned what we were doing, and how come she didn't put up a bigger fuss about you seeing me. The times you kissed me or pulled me close to you and hurt my hair a bit when you did it, I didn't beg you to come back to me those times. And you looked a different kind of uncomfortable, especially when you'd leave.

The weirdest time was when we went to see a movie together, all three of us, *Father of the Bride*, what a crap movie, or maybe it was a cult movie. Anyway afterwards we went to this café in Long Street, and I paid, like I was a visiting aunt, who was loaded, only I wasn't. But I did have a credit card that wasn't maxed out. You didn't have a credit card, neither did she. It's funny how in some situations it's the one person who always pays. You always seemed poor to me, so even though I wasn't loaded, I always paid.

The time we went to see the movie, you sat in the middle. Diane was wearing a long black coat and we had to go to the bathroom together, we didn't talk or anything. We just smiled at each other, like we were each trying to sell something the other didn't really want to buy. The movie was about a wedding, can't remember the details, something about rich Americans who have wedding planners. It was weird to be watching this movie about a wedding, I kept thinking of the three of us sitting there in the dark, and I couldn't concentrate properly, even though you could have got that movie even if you weren't concentrating. I should have told you to piss off, or you should have told me to. I have no idea why she didn't put her foot down. But none of us did in those days. We had this whole notion that you could still be friends afterwards. Now I see it isn't really friends, because there are all these things you can't say, can't admit to. You find you're having several layers of conversations at once. It's like telling lies, you have to keep your story straight and remember what you said, what you are supposed to know and not know. It's not relaxing. Which is one of the main reasons it's not like real friends.

I got to wondering if you ever think about me, and if you ever think about how crazy and fucking sad I was when you left me, that I *spied on you*? It wasn't really spying, more like lying in wait, like a lioness might wait in the trees near a place she knows buck will come to. Okay, no you're right, it was a kind of spying. It cured me of spying though, I felt so freaked out and shaky. And it made me see things a bit differently, I saw how it was between you and her. Even though you sweet-talked me, with some of the stuff that you would say and the way you looked at me, after that spying episode, I had my own version of what was going on. I didn't have to rely on your version. So maybe there was something healthy about what I did. Forced myself to confront what was what. It made me sadder than hell and after that I sort of gave up.

Sometimes I remember those days and it's hard to really connect with why I did certain things. It was all so unbelievably intense and over the top. Compared to those days, I am totally chilled now. I thought about that time we went to see that Athol Fugard play at the Market Theatre, the one set in a school. I picked you up in Rivonia; you were staying with your folks for some weird reason, and I drove there on the M1 way too fast, you were shit scared that I would crash on purpose or something. You kept telling me, "Slow down a bit," not wanting to sound as panicky as you felt. The play was pretty good, calmed me down, took me out of myself, so afterwards I drove properly. I kept the ticket stubs in my jacket pocket for months afterwards, to remind me of you and of my own anguish. You know when you have a sore tooth and you keep feeling it with your tongue, like that. I wanted to feel sad, I didn't want to get over you. Nothing worked out for me with other guys for a long time because I would always talk about you – guaranteed not to make the new guy feel important. But in the end, I did get over you. Just like the songs promise.

# PHONE YOU

The phone is ringing as Jessica gets out of the bath. Her heart jolts as she picks it up. "Hello," she says. There is silence. She waits a moment before replacing the receiver. She feels some fear and resignation as though she deserves this. It was after all adultery, a grim little smile flickers on her face. What a prim word, adultery. The phone rings again. She breathes deeply as she picks it up, "Hello."

"Hi Jess, why don't you come early? We can have a drink before the movie."

"Hi Layla, ...that'd be nice. I'll come ... straight away. Bye." But she holds onto the receiver.

"Is anything the matter?" Layla asks, she too has not put the phone down.

She pauses, "She's still phoning, she just called now."

"We have to think of a way to make her stop."

A few moments later Jessica is in her car driving down Harrow Road. It's a humid Saturday afternoon in November. She's going to a movie with her friends, Layla and Matt, they live together in an old face-brick house in Bez Valley. They are her oldest friends, she's known Matt since High school, he was the head boy of their school. She is closest to Layla whom she met through Matt. Driving relaxes her slightly, even the ten minutes to her friends' home makes a difference. All the robots are green. The traffic is light this afternoon, no sports events on at Ellis Park.

*

She thinks back to a few weeks ago when Lester came to visit her at her flat the first and only time. She'd tidied up, filed bills and letters, put paperclips into a jar; the act of sorting and throwing away the pointless papers that accumulate in her life like leaves in a swimming pool, soothed her When the doorbell rang, she started. For a moment, she wasn't sure who it could be. But it was Lester and she was supposed to be expecting him. He'd phoned on Wednesday to ask if he could come and see her on Saturday afternoon. She'd felt uneasy about it, but agreed.

Most Saturday afternoons she finds herself alone, reading the Weekly Mail from cover to cover, ironing, or listlessly reading a novel on her unmade bed as though her imagination stretches no further than reading. Layla usually gardens on Saturday afternoons, sometimes she phones Jessica and they go to nurseries. Often Matt is busy, as the administrator of Baragwanath Hospital, his work leaves little time for nurseries. Jessica has too much time on her hands. She loves following Layla around as she picks out new shrubs and trees, animatedly describing where she'll plant them. Jessica smiles brightly, even though she can't quite visualize it all. She gulps in the warmth of Layla's voice, listens to her cadences and notices her gestures as she trails after her between lines of potted trees. Sometimes Jessica considers buying a tree or a shrub. She covets the growth of them, the shapes of the leaves, the shadows they cast. On the Saturday she sees Lester, Layla has gone to a new nursery in Broederstroom with Matt, who is unexpectedly free.

*

Her doorbell rings, it's Lester. She opens the door slowly, methodically unlocks the security gate, avoiding looking at him all the while. He enters, her heart sinks as she sees what he's wearing, a waistcoat made from springbok skin.

It's too much for her. She can't possibly go out with him dressed like this. She panics. She has trouble breathing. It reminds her of curios at the Kruger Park, small shields and shoulder bags made from springbok skin. They'd planned to go to Rockey Street for coffee. He notices her staring at the waistcoat. "I've had it since the seventies, I was a supporting musician for the Percy Sledge tour." There is pride in his voice. She pictures six or seven other people in similar waistcoats, wearing white shirts, black pants, it is nighttime, blue and red strobe lights pulse across the audience.

"Aren't you hot?"

"No," he grins and reaches towards her, takes her hand, puts his other hand behind her neck. His eagerness arouses her. He kisses her. She can't respond. She doesn't shut her eyes as he does.

"I can't bear this waistcoat! Please take it off..." She's aware of his bewilderment, "...it's an environmental thing. I'm a vegetarian..." She realises he knows she isn't, "I used to be one, but I still hate skins, they remind me too much of hunting and death and that..." she trails off, feeling ridiculous and cruel.

He takes the waistcoat off in a good-humoured way, folds it and puts it on a chair. "It's okay, I didn't know it'd affect you like that," he takes her hand gently. "Let's go out for that coffee." Jessica is so relieved she feels like crying.

Later they make love, even though she'd decided she wouldn't. It must have been to make up for the waistcoat. She consoles herself by thinking of how to turn the awkward afternoon into a humourous anecdote to tell Layla. She enjoys Lester's body as they make love, his lean energy, his cinnamon skin. She watches the strength and music of his limbs and their movement as if from ten feet away. A rush of desire washes through her, she allows herself to relax into it.

As he dresses, the phone rings. Jessica picks it up. A woman asks, "Is Lester there?"

"Yes," she wishes she'd said no. She knows immediately who it is. "I'll call him." She puts her hand over the mouthpiece. "It's for you. A woman." She sees the easiness in his manner evaporate.

"You should've said I'm not here," he whispers.

"Too late."

That was the first call. Now she's had possibly eighty. Lester's wife began a campaign of harassing her. Jessica takes to unplugging the phone at night before she goes to sleep.

She finds the situation bizarre and at times even funny, with all its clichés of encountering a vengeful jealous wife. The only thing missing is the murdered pet rabbit. At least I don't have animals or children, she thinks. She checks her car tyres frequently, and keeps an eye on her rearview mirror while driving, to see that she isn't being followed.

She endures several embarrassing phone calls at work, in which a man leaves messages with Lydia, the first one was: "The man you met in Hillbrow on Friday night, says he went to the doctor today, the tests were positive." She doesn't know whether to laugh or scream when she reads the message in Lydia's tight, competent handwriting. She decides to adopt the silent approach. She's aware of Lydia expecting her to confide, to explain. She says nothing. She's sure that the other women in Admin have heard about the messages.

*

Lester and Jessica met during a two-week project management course for people involved in housing development work held at Natal University in Durban in late November the previous year. There were over a hundred participants from different parts of the country, all staying in student residences. The academic year was over, the residences empty apart from those on the course.

She was attracted to Lester straight away, he was quiet and reserved. She liked the bright prints of his handmade pants. He smiled easily and seemed preoccupied with inward things. She caught his eyes looking at her several times before they both smiled and introduced themselves. The first time they spoke he told her he was married.

Jessica liked rising early and swimming lengths in the pool a couple of blocks away from her room. She delighted in the lush forest around the residences, the unfamiliar birdcalls, the smell of damp vegetation and tropical flowers heavy in the air. Lester discovered that she swam at a time when others were still asleep. He took to swimming in the early morning too.

Wherever Jessica looked there was Lester, smiling at her, saying little, watching her. She responded to him, liking his companionable silence. He was a musician and moved as though his body was a musical instrument. All this charmed Jessica and she let down her reserve. Within a few days she found herself in the middle of an erotic encounter that had as much to do with the place as with the two people. She was amazed she had gotten involved with a married man. She was thrilled by the illicitness of it, his being married, her being white and him black.

He told her how he'd built his house himself, including the bricklaying, the plumbing, and the carpentry. He told her of his two sons and his three-year old daughter, Phyllis. Later in thinking about the affair she decided that it was the unstructured time, the release from her routine, the caress of the sultry nights, the drinking more than usual that invited her to behave in a way that she wouldn't normally have. She felt the need to explain it to herself, to rationalize having an affair with a married man.

His wife phoned one evening while they were lying on the narrow bed in his room. They'd been lying silently caressing each other's arms and faces, drifting in and out of sleep. Someone called

Lester to the phone. He'd pulled on a pair of shorts and a crumpled shirt and gone to speak to her. When he returned he told her his wife had discovered condoms in Elliot's school bag (he was the sixteen year old son). Jessica wondered what she was doing looking in the school bag. She didn't listen to Lester's words. She listened to his voice, the proud laughter as he spoke about his family.

Part of the pleasure for Jessica of being with Lester was the privacy of it, they weren't a couple. She didn't have to surrender all her time, her identity to him. Because he was married, they didn't appear in public together. It was a relief to her, she liked being alone. They spoke at tea, and ate lunch together sometimes, but for the most part they only saw each other in the dark or in the swimming pool. On the last night of the workshop, Lester told Jessica that he loved her and that he wanted to leave his wife, and move in with her.

She was speechless. She couldn't even begin to explain to him how unlikely and impossible this seemed to her. She imagined her small flat, hardly even big enough for her. He'd have to drive to Krugersdorp where he worked, she wondered what the traffic would be like. She pictured his three children sleeping in the lounge when they visited for weekends. She thought of his house, the one he'd built with his own hands. She saw his wife pacing from room to room, angry and hurt, or lying on their double bed weeping, cooking supper for the children, her face pale and drawn, snapping at them. Jessica pitied Elliot, the one with the condoms, she'd take it out on him. Like father like son. "No, Lester, you're married, you've got children," was all she could say. She couldn't find the words to express the consequences she could see flowing from his words. "It's been lovely, being with you, but I can't love you. It would never work. Our lives are too different and we're too deep into them," she heard herself say. Although this wasn't it, wasn't the real reason. He didn't say anything, looked at her like a dog deprived of its walk.

"I think I'll go back to my room tonight," she said quietly.

He reached for her, she could see his eyes moisten. She felt sad, weighed down by a heaviness, a carpet across her shoulders. She sensed Lester's relief as she stood up, pulled her arm away.

Later she wondered if he felt he had to declare his love, that somehow the occasion demanded it, that it was the polite thing to do. She imagined how he would have regretted his declaration in the weeks that followed if she'd readily accepted.

*

After several weeks of the phone harassment, Layla insists on Jessica changing her phone number. It is Saturday morning, they are sitting inside Nino's having coffee. The streets of Braamfontein are empty on weekends. They have both found parking right outside, which means they can keep an eye on their cars. "I think I'm going to take out a restraining order against this woman. I just want her to leave me alone." Jessica is showing signs of strain. Tears come too easily.

"They probably won't be able to do anything. Or won't, even if they can, but I'll come with you," Layla offers, as she sips her second cappuccino.

The visit to the police station in Yeoville is a farce. They walk across the park, it's a windy afternoon. In the summer she walks this way to the pool before work to swim twenty lengths. She has only been in the police station once before, she cannot even remember why. It was years ago. The sight of the police station always tightens her heart, as do the yellow vans she often sees driving around her neighbourhood streets.

There are two policemen sitting behind the high wooden counter, they're talking idly to each other in Zulu. There is no one else in the charge office when they get there. "I'd like to take out a restraining order against someone who's been harassing me."

The two men slowly turn to look at her; they're still talking to each other. They looked mildly interested.

"Do you know who the person is?" one of the men asks her as he picks up a pen and pulls a printed buff folder towards him. He doesn't look at her.

"Yes, Ivy Pienaar."

"How's she harassing you?" He starts writing on the folder.

"She phones me constantly all night. She leaves rude messages at work, and I think she's having me followed." She feels Layla's surprise, she hasn't told her this bit.

"How do you know it's her who's harassing you? Does she identify herself when she calls?"

"No."

"How do you know it's her?" He has stopped writing and waits for her answer.

She looks behind her, there are now four or five people in the charge office, she hasn't been aware of them entering. She lowers her voice, "I had an affair with her husband." The man who has been questioning her raises his eyebrows. She imagines she can read his thoughts. Well you deserve this then, don't you? He mutters under his breath in Zulu to the other policeman. They both laugh. Jessica feels herself blushing.

"Where does this woman live?"

"In Krugersdorp."

"It's not in our jurisdiction. You will have to go to Krugersdorp and lay the charge there." He pauses. "Are you still having this affair with her husband?" he asks loudly.

Layla intervenes, "Could we continue this discussion in a private interviewing room?"

The policemen don't answer for a few moments. At last, the questioner stands up, "Follow me." He emerges from behind the counter, and opens a door into a room off the charge office foyer, "In here." He shuts the door, leaves them alone. They sit down next to each other.

At first they are silent and then they both start laughing and are almost unable to stop even when a policewoman enters the room carrying a blue folder and a pen. As the interview proceeds, Jessica knows that it's pointless. It isn't going to work, the legal systems aren't in place to enforce a restraining order. She will have her phone number changed, and the next time the phone rings at home and she has to listen to silence she's going to tell Lester's wife that she's laid a restraining order against her and that if she's harassed in any way ever again, the police will pay her a visit. She suspects that this will be enough to frighten the woman into leaving her alone. She feels oddly guilty about this threat and feels little satisfaction when she does speak in this way to Lester's wife that same night.

She is out all day Sunday, and on Monday Telkom swiftly changes her number. Their efficiency surprises her. She tells the man she speaks to that she's being harassed, "I live alone, I need to be able to use my phone at night." He murmurs sympathetically, asks her to wait a few moments, and then gives Jessica her new phone number that is immediately active. All she has to do now is let Layla, her family and other friends know the new number.

As the weeks go by, she becomes more relaxed, less vigilant, the sound of her phone ringing doesn't cause her heart to contract, her breathing to change. She still feels some relief when it's a voice rather than the malignant silence.

Almost a year after her number was changed Jessica bumps into Lester at a seminar at the Balalaika. She sees him across the room before he sees her. She sighs. Later they speak somewhat stiffly. After a few moments, he asks how she is, how she's been. His voice is soft and tender. She says nothing. She doesn't ask after him or his family.

"I'd love to see you sometime," he says.

"Oh Lester, you're too much," she laughs.

"Can't I even phone you?"

# Warm enough

Do you remember that weird time in about '92? Before the elections. There was a bit of a light at the end of the tunnel. Anyway you must remember my friend, Ruth – I bet you never heard that she had an affair with my brother, Grant? Ja, it wasn't for that long, a couple of months at most. Anyway it was when he was a clown in a play at the Market Theatre, did you ever see it? So he got really trashed on something, white pipes, I don't even know, I was never that au fait with all the options. Ja, apparently he couldn't sleep for two weeks and he disappeared with the clown suit. No one knew where he was. Later we heard he'd been painting garden furniture at a friend's parents' place somewhere out at Fourways or Lanseria, and talking about becoming a tennis coach. He even spoke of getting an Arthur Ashe tennis racquet. Ruth was the only one who spoke to him while he was lost. And she believed him, she believed all the tennis coach stuff and she encouraged him. He sounded so convincing. Passionate, knowledgeable – you remember what he was like? I would have laughed at him if he'd told me that tennis coach shit. Except I would probably have cried instead.

So they had to cancel the play because there was no understudy and no extra costumes. It was some kind of improv play that had been his idea in the first place. Ag shame man, Grant's name was mud with those okes, as you can imagine, for years, not just months. Some of the other actors in that play went on to star in big shot TV series like the one about Barney Barnato and *Isidingo* even. Grant was a brilliant actor when he wasn't drugging, I always felt sad for him, he could have also been famous and that.

So anyway after the whole clown fiasco, Grant spent a couple of years on the streets, in Yeoville and then in Cape Town. I even heard from someone that he tried to score free Kentucky from one of his army mates who worked at KFC head office. He phoned the oke from a tickey box. Remember how there used to be tickey boxes hey? The oke pretended he didn't know Grant, how blind is that? Even my Mom didn't hear from him for at least a year.

Poor Ruth was a bit in love with him for a while; he was so sweet and fucked up, and he played the guitar and sang to her and made romantic gestures with flowers. He rode a motorbike, nothing fancy, just a Honda 250 or something like that, and he had this amazing World War II jacket he'd got from my grandpa. My grandpa was in Monty's army in North Africa. Grant wore it all the time, it was the Real McCoy, he always had a soft spot for family memorabilia. And old Grant, he knew how to spin a line hey. The gift of the gab, my Gran used to say. When he was a kid all his teachers loved him, even though he was a cheeky little bugger.

Ruth had just broken up with Nathan when she got involved with Grant. Nathan was one of those single-minded okes, funny and bright, quick witted. Sports-mad. Ag, in the end it had all got too intense for her with him. She began to wonder if the main reason he was with her was because her father was a famous political lawyer and he was hoping it would rub off on him. Ja, anyway, the next thing was, Nathan and I started sleeping together. I can't even remember how it happened. It was like comfort eating. Suddenly you wake up and you smell the roses or should I say donuts. One day it seemed like – there he was, I woke up and there he was, Nathan was in my bed. I remember some uptight friend of mine saying at the time that my bed was like a railway station. She really cheesed me off. Why is it better to only ever have slept with one or two men? Can you tell me? Look, I was being kind to Nathan. He was very cut up about Ruth. When we were alone he was sweet like some dogs are, you know golden retrievers, sort of soppy and well meaning. I couldn't bear to see how sad he was, and I wasn't involved with anyone else. And he and Ruth had broken up. So it wasn't completely wrong?

Anyhow when Nathan heard about Grant and Ruth, he was over to Ruth's like a shot. I was the kiepie who told him. Fuck, I wish I'd kept my mouth shut. So Grant and Ruth and Nathan had one of those B-movie scenes, only it happened in Muller Street. Grant climbed out of Ruth's bedroom window onto the balcony, he was in his underpants and he sat there while Ruth and Nathan argued with each other in the lounge. Ruth didn't really want Nathan to know that she and Grant were kafoofling in the middle of the day. I suppose she didn't really want Nathan to know about Grant at all. That is the thing I feel the most shit about, even now, when I think back. I mean Ruth was my friend. Ja, so Nathan didn't know Grant was right there. Luckily Grant was stoned enough to be fairly cool about sitting outside on the balcony half naked. They fought for so long he even fell asleep out there, or so he told me.

Grant lived in a flat at the bottom end of Dunbar Street. You didn't ever see his flat did you? I only went there a couple of times. And the one time I visited him there he'd filled his whole flat with branches he'd brought in from when the Council pruned the plane trees in his road. He was so mal, hey. Bos bevok. He didn't want to leave them there to die in the street like rubbish, he said. His place spaced me out, completely. Apart from the branches, which was enough to push me over the edge, his flat was dirty and I mean vuil, hey. Dishes and pizza boxes and crusty pots rotting all over the place and I'm not exaggerating. Stompies and bottlenecks – not even in ashtrays. The oke was living like an animal. I was glad my old lady couldn't see how he was living, she would have turned in her grave. Well she isn't dead yet, but you know what I mean. No furniture apart from the mattress and sheets and blankets so filthy you couldn't tell what colour they were originally. It was worse than bergies, and that's saying something. I couldn't stop myself from tuning him, "Sies man Grant, how can you live like this? Are you a dog?" But you know what? Not even dogs, not even pigs live like that.

Old Grant was always such a joker, so full of life and laughs, I felt like a dried up old prune around him, even when we were kids. He could always make you hose yourself. But I'm sorry, that flat was the end for me. Something inside me tightened. It scared me. I don't think Ruth ever went there, she would have run a mile. Grant used to visit her in his leather jacket, somehow emerging from that bloody pig sty cleaned up enough for a person like Ruth to be cool with. No you've got to hand it to the oke, he's pulled off some tricks in his day and getting involved with Ruth was one of those occasions – big time.

In any case, Ruth and I were never close again. I suppose she didn't trust me after all of that shit went down. I still think about her sometimes, miss her even, but in the end there was too much water under the bridge. Nathan, the dweezil, told Ruth about his 'fling' with me as a way of tuning her for Grant. Jissus we were all so dof. Look it didn't help him, Ruth never forgave him for that, nor me. Things between Grant and Ruth also cooled off, she lost interest, she was too cut up about everything. Grant was pretty freaked too; he really dug Ruth. She was older than him, and she was very pretty and soft and they'd had this lekker playful thing going between them. She was probably the classiest chick he'd ever got near.

I remember this one night, we were all at Dawson's. It was before Ruth and Nathan split up, she and I were still friends and somehow Grant came along for the ride that night. He used to pitch up at my place when he wanted something to eat and he couldn't come up with a better plan. One time when he couldn't find me he ate loquats from one of those big gardens in Jan Smuts near the Zoo, where the trees hang over onto the pavement. Anyway I think that was when they met, Grant and Ruth. The Radio Rats were making a comeback and Dawson's was cooking. People like James Phillips and Johannes Kerkorrel showed up. Definitely the best jol in Joburg that night. We all danced like mal, even Nathan, who wasn't really a dancer. His heart wasn't in it, but that night he was jiving with the best of us. That journalist who got shot a few months later in Katlehong was there too. Everybody was at Dawson's, even the short drug dealer who always wore that mustard-yellow felt homburg. When I think about it now, it was like we were celebrating the end of something terrible that we'd lived through our whole lives. It was like the war was over and who the fuck knew what would happen next?

After everything cooled down between the four of us, Nathan and I still slept together sometimes. He would drive past my flat, down Kenmere Road on his way home. He lived up in those larney flats behind the water tower. If my lights were on he'd phone from his place. It was before cell phones.

The conversation would go something like this,
"Howzit. Are you there?"
"Ja."
"What're you doing?"
"Reading."
"Are you warm enough?"
"Almost."

A few minutes later he'd be there, smiling and as pleased as all hell with himself, at my door. We would usually fuck and then curl up and sleep tightly wrapped together. Those nights with Nathan were quite lekker, a bit less lonely, you know. The mornings were sometimes a bit awkward. Deep down I knew I wanted more than a bit on the side here and there. One night I said, "Ja, I am," when he asked, "Are you warm enough?" and then he didn't call again. Just like that. Can you believe it?

The next time I bumped into him he was dropping a video into the slot at that shop in Parktown North with his four-year-old daughter. I was living down the road in Blairgowrie. Married and everything. But that's another story. She was only cute hey, his daughter, big blue eyes and wild, curly blonde hair. I couldn't believe it, almost. If I hadn't seen her with my own eyes. Somehow I'd never pictured any of us jollers with kids and all of that. He was a hotshot corporate lawyer about to emigrate to Canada.

I haven't seen Ruth for years. Sometimes I hear about her, what she's doing from mutual friends. The weird thing is that she also lives in Canada. She makes really short documentary films. I don't know if she ever got married or anything.

Grant opened up a video shop in Mossel Bay with his wife, Jeannie. I don't know where he met her, I'm too scared to ask. How she tamed him, your guess is as good as mine. But the life down there suits him (rather him than me – hey?) He fishes and surfs quite a bit. Drinks every night. But not too much. They take it in turns at the shop. He fetches and carries the kids, they've got two beautiful little girls and can you believe it – he designs websites in his spare time as a sort of a cross between a hobby and a job. He was always someone who was going to be able to reinvent himself. It's not a bad life. Oh and he also has a fucking conspiracy theory blog, most of which he makes up himself.

Anyway I better dash. You look great, next time you must tell me all about where you've been.

# LOOKING FOR TROUBLE

To tell the truth, when Patrick hit me that time, in my face, I wasn't surprised. I wasn't exactly expecting it, but I was expecting something, and after that the dread stopped. We'd been seeing each other for about a year, in an on-off fashion. Afterwards I kept thinking I should have known, I should have been able to prevent it from happening.

I met Patrick at a party I only went to by chance. I'd bumped into Chris, who I hadn't seen for ages, not since third year at Wits. I was browsing at Exclusive Books in Rosebank, I used to spend all my spare cash on books. I'd been to an early movie and was meeting Tina at ten, so I was killing time. After he invited me to the party, I almost didn't go, but then I decided that I'd better. You better get out there and try to meet people, was the voice I listened to. I already had this arrangement with Tina to go to a gig at the Market Theatre; she was pissed off with me for not staying for the whole thing. Mahlatini and the Mahotella Queens were playing and some other performers, and it would be a good jol, dancing and everything. I think Tina was most put out because we went in separate cars, she always had this big issue with driving around alone after dark.

In any case it was me who had the near-hijacking experience. Very damn close. These two young black guys ambled towards my car. I got in and locked the door, thinking to myself all the time that I was being paranoid. Next thing they were grabbing the door handles and shaking the car. I managed to pull away and they banged the window as I drove off. All the way to Greenside my heart was pounding, and I was swearing out loud. I hardly paid attention to where I was going.

I got to the party and I didn't know anyone except for Chris, who was otherwise occupied, I didn't care. I poured myself a whisky, and was just settling down on the stairs to have a quiet drink, calm my nerves, when Patrick came up to me and before I could stop myself I was telling him what had happened. "I don't know how come I didn't panic, and didn't stall, my car's such an old skedonk. I was terrified one of them might pull the door off."

"It's all right. It's over now," Patrick said, his voice low and soothing.

"The weird thing is I don't think they really are hijackers. They looked too young. Maybe seventeen. I think they spotted me and thought they would give it a try. Maybe they just thought they would have it for themselves. The chop shops would laugh, if they had brought my old Escort in. Sorry, I'm raving… I was late and Tina, my friend, was waiting for me. I just grabbed the first parking I could find. I forgot it was going to be dark by the time I got back to the car. I don't even know why I came to this party. I hate parties. But I feel I have to go to them, because otherwise…" I wasn't sure how to finish the sentence without giving myself away. "Well, otherwise, I'd spend too much time working."

"Come on sweetheart, try to stop thinking about it," he smiled at me, touching my arm gently. I liked it that he called me sweetheart, even though we'd only just met. Tina wouldn't have trusted that about him, but it felt like something I could sink into after my earlier terror.

"Yeah, you're right. I better go. I'm completely whacked." I put down my empty glass, still crunching the ice. I didn't even say goodbye to Chris, because I wasn't sure how I'd drive home if I stayed any longer. Patrick and I didn't exchange numbers afterwards. I didn't want to phone Chris to ask, so I just left it at that. But I couldn't get him out of my mind. He was a small man, with dark hair and eyes that danced, as though he had some private joke that kept him amused. And this gentle solicitous manner. He was in his early forties, almost ten years older than me, which appealed to me as though it was glamorous.

The next time I saw him was a few months later at one of those dark, boozy Yeoville parties, too many people crammed into a small flat. I'd been invited third hand, and rather than stay in bed reading, I went along. The saving grace of this party was the rooftop, standing up there, looking out at the city lights strung as far as you could see in any direction. Ponte, the Hillbrow tower soaring higher than the others. I knew it was the best jol that night because the short black drug dealer who always wore the yellow felt homburg was there, and all the trendiest trendies were there. I'd been dancing by myself in the lounge. I pretended not to notice when Patrick came up behind me and put his hands on my hips, then slipped them into the back pockets of my jeans. He danced in this way with me for several songs without speaking, turning me and gliding his hands round my waist and back as he did so. It was the only time he ever danced with me, a ploy to get me into bed. We moved to the rooftop, both drinking Black Label from the bottle. He started to kiss my neck and grip my hair firmly but gently, it wasn't long before I left the party in his car and went to his flat. It was not something I usually did. But lately I'd found myself behaving more and more recklessly, as though I was looking for trouble.

We started having an affair, it was never "a relationship", it never felt like it was going anywhere. He was a journalist, a foreign correspondent for Reuters. He had only recently returned to South Africa. Most of the people I knew were teachers or academics like me or worked in NGOs of one kind or another.

His flat was austere, with only one bookcase filled with books by German philosophers and economics books, there were only six or so novels, two by JM Coetzee. He had lots of plants on his balcony, and a few indoor plants. There were no paintings on the walls, no ornaments, no *tsatskes*. He had black Venetian blinds at his bedroom window. Minimalist, he called it.

*

My block of flats had been built in the 1930s, a small two storey block, I knew all the neighbours by sight. The landlady had recently installed a security gate on the front door and at the garage. There was no buzzer. Friends had to phone ahead or stand on the pavement and shout, "Jenna, Jenna." I would lean over from my balcony and throw the key down, but mostly I would run downstairs and let them in, the exercise was good for me.

From the beginning, Patrick used to turn up outside my door. "Do you want to come for a walk?" Sometimes I wouldn't have seen him for weeks, and once it was even a couple of months. He'd suddenly be there, unannounced, smiling. I always agreed to whatever he suggested. Nothing I was busy with seemed important enough not to drop, it was usually writing a paper, or some endless marking. I would grab my costume or a jacket, some money, put on my shoes and go for a swim, a coffee, a drink, supper, whatever it was he offered. I liked those silent drives and walks through Houghton and the Wilds or Delta Park, places I would never go to on my own. They weren't safe. Everyone had stories of muggings, and worse.

Mostly when we spent the night together it would be at his flat. On his futon, with its clean white sheets. No-one knows where I am, I would think. He was such a particular man, his cupboards were all neatly arranged. He did all his own cleaning and ironing, very unusual for a white South African man. He didn't even have a char once a week. He'd lived abroad for many years.

Sometimes he would talk, tell me about when he lived in a squat in London or when he drove a taxi in New York. Or what it had been like to be a scholarship boy at Bishops. I listened and didn't say much myself, my own stories and anecdotes stillborn inside me as I listened, fitting myself to him. I kept hoping he would become more predictable, and that I could start to rely on having him in my life. But he made sure it was never like that. He came and went as it suited him, only phoning when he wanted to, returning the messages I left on his pager occasionally. As soon as I found myself getting used to him, he would disappear.

I was on edge, passing time, making arrangements with friends that I hoped I would cancel. Mostly I didn't cancel, and would go to the new art movie at Rosebank or whatever I'd planned to do. One evening when Tina and I had a drink at Times Square, I sipped my brandy and hot chocolate, and listened to her describe her plans to sell up and go to London. Tina kept trying to persuade me to give up on Patrick. I would agree. Till the next time he appeared at my door. All the while a growing unease built up inside me. I knew that something terrible was going to happen. I just didn't know what it was or how to stop it. I became obsessed with the Yeoville rapist to the extent that I slept with my windows closed, even on hot nights. I listened at length to all the stories of the rapist that were doing the rounds. Sometimes I'd wake up at two or three in the morning. Convinced there was danger lurking in my flat, I would get up and look into all the rooms, behind the furniture, in my cupboards. When I was satisfied I was alone, I would get back into bed, and sleep restlessly.

*

The final showdown happened on a Sunday, after Easter, I walked over to Patrick's flat, I still remember what I was wearing, a pale blue t-shirt and white cotton shorts, my running shoes. He was sitting in the armchair in his lounge, slumped in a way that made him look even smaller. He looked defeated, but with an odd tension in his body as though he might spring out of the chair and do something unexpected. The chair was a non-descript, navy blue cotton weave chair. I stood looking down at him, quivering with rage and passion, "You have to stop this… thing of coming and going as it suits you. Go or stay, but you can't do both. Just stop it." Patrick sat there, said little as if he was totally unaffected by what I was saying.

I got so worked up and desperate to get some reaction out of him. I looked around, frantic to do something. I swept an African violet in a pot plant off the table next to me.

"My mother gave me that!" he shouted, his jaw tight. The pot was in shards, soil all over the floor, the purple flowers peeking through the debris.

Before I could see what I'd done (it was only later replaying what had happened that I saw the pot, the soil, the flowers) he leapt up and hit me. Not once, but three times, in the face. I didn't make a sound. I heard bone and cartilage connecting, a sickening sound, and then slumped to the floor, blood spewing everywhere, tears streaming down my face. I put my forehead on my arm, and stayed like that.

After some time he approached me. "Get away from me. Don't touch me. Don't come near me."

I remember washing my face, and the red pouring down the drain. So much blood.

He left to fetch me some clothes, the ones I was wearing were soaked in blood. In that time I phoned Frank, my dearest friend.

I knew Frank would take me in, and make it as alright as it could be. I couldn't face phoning Tina. I was afraid she would blame me because I'd hung in with Patrick, even though they'd both told me he was no good. "I'll get him to bring me over," I told Frank. He wrote down Patrick's address in case I didn't get to his place by six. Later I was glad I'd phoned Frank, because some part of me wanted to forgive Patrick and pretend that nothing had happened. I was tempted to crawl into bed with him and have him hold me while I fell asleep. The phone call was a chink of light in my thoughts, I knew Frank was worried about me and would be waiting for me. It forced the next thing to happen, it meant I had to step away from Patrick and his flat, the mess in the lounge, I had to look at myself and see it was over. We'd broken something that could never be fixed. I felt cold.

After Patrick came back from my flat with clean clothes, before he took me to Frank's, we spoke about what had happened. I watched him clean the floor with a cloth, rinsing it in a bucket. My blood, I thought.

"I'm so sorry. I don't know what came over me, where this came from. I know you will never forgive me." I had already forgiven him, but I also knew I had to get away from him, even though I wanted to stay.

I should have seen it coming, I kept thinking. Not straight away, but quite early on, if only I'd been alert, awake to what was going on, I could have recognized the signs. Why wasn't I overwhelmed with the danger signals?

Like me, Patrick lived in Yeoville, we used to swim together early in the morning before work or on hot afternoons after work at the public pool. I remember a particular day, we had driven across town to Melville for a change. I sat on the concrete steps next to the pool, I'd swum my 20 laps. Patrick was still in the pool, his eyes insect-like in the black goggles. He always swam at least 80 laps. I closed my eyes, lifted my face to the sun. I could hear the shrieks of children amplified by the water. Patrick swam all his laps in crawl, while I started off in crawl, switched to breaststroke and finished off with a last lap in butterfly. "Showing off," Patrick teased me, more than once. On this day he stopped in his middle lane, a swarm of children in his way. His face was clenched. He looked up, saw me watching, smiled and waved. I breathed a deep sigh. He shook the water off his body like a dog as he emerged from the pool. I always smiled to see his tiny black Speedo and the easy way he walked around the pool to where I was sitting to pick up his towel. I always left my towel as close to the metal steps as I could. He wet me as he shook his head. "Let's go for a drink."

"OK," he kissed the back of my sun-warmed neck. I didn't ask him how many laps he swam, even though I wanted to.

In the days after he hit me, I felt as though my mind was working overtime, I couldn't stop thinking about incidents between us that now frightened me, as though I'd only begun to hear the ominous soundtrack that had been playing all along.

I remembered how he chased me with a squashed dead grasshopper, laughing at me. It was a biggish, green, dead one. Dried out. I noticed it lying on the windowsill while we were having breakfast. I wondered how it got there, up to his fifth floor flat. Patrick came and stood next to me, suddenly he grabbed the grasshopper and thrust it at me, I panicked and screamed. I could feel my heart beating faster and my face flush. I wanted to get away from him and the insect, but I was trapped. I started to cry and sat down on the floor. I told him to fuck off. "What's wrong with you?" I asked him. He stood there looking at me as though I was spoiling his fun.

One night we both nearly got shot, we were walking around Yeoville in the dark. Several shots were fired a few feet away from us. He flung me to the ground on the pavement behind a car. We waited for ten minutes maybe. Till the screams had stopped. A man was lying dead in the street, we heard the police sirens approaching, we left the scene. I can't blame him, but that was the kind of thing that seemed to happen when I was with him.

He slapped me once while we were making love or should I say, while we were having sex, he told me, "Women like it if you're gentle, then later you can be a bit rough," as though he had let me in on a secret. I felt distant from what he had said, unimplicated, as though he wasn't talking about me.

Another time he invited me to his place for supper. When I got there he was already drunk. He almost burnt the panzarotti and the red pepper and tomato sauce he was making. He flew into a rage and threw several of his white dinner plates and the contents of the saucepan onto the kitchen floor. As we drove across town to a restaurant in Melville to make up for the disaster, all I could think of was seeing him on his hands and knees as he cleaned up this white pasta and red sauce all over the floor. He filled a bucket with warm soapy water and a cloth, wiping up the red mess. Rinsing the cloth, wiping until all traces of his outburst had been cleaned up. I stood there, watching.

As I drove back to my flat from Frank's place, I wondered, Do all these pieces come from the same jigsaw box? I kept thinking, Was I asking for it? As though, if I looked at what happened through a different prism, I would get a different answer, discover a different story. Sometimes I wonder if he knocked some sense into me, because I couldn't understand why I had kept going back for more when he didn't treat me right.

Sometimes when I tried to talk to him about what wasn't working for me, it was as though I was hearing a voice-over, as though somebody else was talking and I wasn't even in the room.

A few days before the incident, I was driving down Louis Botha, I spotted his metallic blue Golf parked outside the Radium. I stopped off, he was drinking a beer and watching the cricket, England playing Pakistan. He bought me a beer and fish and chips, and was pleased to see me. I felt so happy that afternoon, as though I had a real relationship and as though it might all work out after all.

*

I learnt that it takes three weeks for bruises to heal. In a picture Frank took, about a month later, we'd gone to the Magaliesberg one Sunday for a picnic, I can still see the ghosts of the bruises. I look like a woman who is tired or is recovering from a life threatening illness. I start to see other women with bruises. It was not something I had noticed before. Women of all shapes and sizes and races have bruises on their faces. I recognize their awkwardness and shame. Once or twice I have wanted to say something, but what? I see you?

Sometimes I circle back to the bruise Patrick gave me. I think of how as a child I liked bruises, they were badges of honour, something to return to, to contemplate. If you poked them, they would hurt a little, as the bruise faded, changing colour magically from purple to green, so would the hurting. You could show bruises off to friends, get a cuddle from your mother, it was evidence that you had been hurt, and that you had survived the hurt.

Other hurts, grief, disappointment, betrayal, live in the dark – there is nothing to show, nothing to point to.

Bruises came from falls and bumps, from rushing and climbing and colliding. They were from being busy and alive, from riding bikes, jumping out of trees. I never got a bruise from a person, until I was an adult woman. It was not a bruise I was proud of.

One night at Times Square, I was wearing a loose white cotton dress and my suede jacket, my legs bare. He was drinking whisky. I loved living in Yeoville, the short walk to Rockey Street. That night we wandered street after street in the dark, admiring the Art Deco features in the lobbies of blocks of flats.

Sometimes I still think about how warm and scented the air was, and how it was an adventure to be making this private inventory of architectural details. No one can take away the past, what people have meant to each other. Sometimes I wonder if he ever thinks of me, if he hates me or is still sorry. We had a sexual magic, does he still think of that? He suffered a public humiliation because of what happened, because of what he did to me. Chris, our mutual friend, told all his friends, his crowd. It was different for me, but all the same it left shame in me, lodged in my body.

I liked it when Patrick had been in my bed, I used to find hairs from his beard on my sheets. Sometimes when you make love with someone, you get hair in your mouth, its one of those surprising things that no one mentions, not even in books.

I didn't expect to lose him for good. I can't have him back, and none of it has gone away. I still feel the hard pebble, somewhere deep inside. I dream I am a dead woman made of straw who comes to life. I dream my mother gives me a mechanical bull for my birthday. I dream I live in a glass flat in a tall building, and the sun streams into my lounge, until it is too hot.

# Plumbing – a short history

A series of men tried to fix the dripping cold-water bath tap in my flat. Only one of them was a plumber, he was sent by Mrs Levin, the landlady. He was a bit overweight, dressed in black pants and white short-sleeved shirt, a Hasidic man with a big beard. He didn't say much and I got the feeling he didn't like me watching him as he worked. He took the bath taps apart, replaced the washers and used white plumber's ribbon tape. The tap didn't drip for several months after he'd attended to it.

Then Nico tried – softly spoken, tall Nico. We were both working on our dissertations (his was in Archeology, mine in Classics) when the matter of my dripping tap came up. He was sharing a house with my friends, Simon and Jonathan, in Bedford Street. I was using Simon's computer, and Nico was working on his own, in the same study. It was still in the days of WordStar 2000. We both had season tickets for the Yeoville pool. It was summer, days that felt they'd be better spent out of doors, at the pool in fact, where we often went for a 'short' break. Nico said he'd come and have a look at my tap, see what he could do. We didn't notice the tap in the bathroom that switched off only the water to my flat, so he turned the whole building's water off. It was a weekday morning. Fortunately most people in the building were at work. He wielded a large shifting spanner. At the time I thought it was a monkey wrench. He changed the washers after dismantling both taps, water gushed everywhere. He also tightened something. He looked so efficient and able-bodied and large, ducked in under the over-sized geyser, half squatting in the bath.

Tim also tried. I was madly attracted to him. Tim was a computer analyst, he drove a Ford Bantam bakkie, and was the coolest, trendiest person I'd ever known. He was the first person I ever saw wearing those Clark Kent type black-framed glasses. He was bright and a bit broken, full of talk and smiles, which went a long way to covering up the emptiness and sadness. He brought along an awe-inspiring tool kit. I'd taken the day off work for the occasion. We got into bed first, and then had breakfast. Then he undid the taps and made his diagnosis, which involved a trip to Yeoville Hardware for the white plumber's tape and clear gel that hardens into a plastic consistency.

When we got back he did various things to the taps, after which we climbed into bed again, and then fell asleep. When we woke it was about half past three. There was something desolate about the afternoon, Tim's tools scattered all around the floor, the weak winter light.

We dressed and went for a beer at Rockafellas. I so wanted to love him, yet I resisted. Even when he appeared at work one day, kissed me in the marble foyer in front of the security guard, three Italian chocolates in a brown paper bag for me, I resisted. About six months later he emigrated to Auckland.

Gilbert also tried to fix the tap. His attempt also involved a trip to Yeoville Hardware. I'm not sure what we bought. He had a small bag of tools in his white Nissan Sentra. I met him on a study trip to the United States sponsored by the US government. He was married, and had three children. His wife found out about the affair and mounted a campaign which was the personal equivalent of 'desert storm' to terrorise me into giving him up. This was overkill on her part, as I wasn't trying to hold onto him. She seemed to want to frighten me into utter humiliation and fear, to prevent me from ever doing anything like that again. I often wonder what punishment she dreamt up for him? The Gilbert story is a much longer story, I won't go into it here, save to say the tap stopped dripping for about three weeks.

It made me feel guilty. Once I left the plug in the bath by mistake, when I came home a few hours later the bath was half full. I felt guilty about all the water that was being wasted. At nights when I couldn't sleep, I'd hear the tap drip. Eventually I'd get out of bed and position the hand-shower hose so the drop of water fell onto it, cushioning the noise.

Patrick also attempted to fix the tap. He worked for Reuters. He was a small man, nearly ten years older than me, his hair prematurely grey. He carried a bleeper at all times, and had to read all the papers every day. There were phone calls in the middle of the night. It was 1993 and early 1994 when he was in my life, there was a lot going on just before the first democratic elections. It was thrilling, glamorous even, knowing the inside stories on the news in those years, like where Winnie was on a particular night and what she was up to.

He bought washers in several sizes from Yeoville Hardware. We had to make at least three trips. It was hot walking to and from the hardware shop. It must have been November, the jacarandas were blooming and the grass in the park was green. Another time we went to a different shop on Louis Botha. But I think that was to buy paint. I decided to paint my flat, but only ever got as far as the entrance hall. That was later after I'd met Steve and had decided to move to the Eastern Cape. Steve didn't even consider fixing the tap. After all I was moving to live with him. All his taps worked. And besides he didn't have a bath.

When I moved out of the flat, the tap still dripped. The block of flats was built in the 1940s. There were some art deco light fittings and bathroom tiles. The only way the dripping was going to stop was if the taps were replaced and the plumbing redone. The wiring could have been redone too. Several of the lights didn't work even if you replaced the bulbs. One morning the kettle and toaster plug smoked in an alarming way, the smell of burning electrical wires was even more alarming. That time Mrs Levin got an electrician in; he did a minor rewiring job, and replaced the wall plug in the kitchen. It drew attention to the smoke-blackened patch around the plug. You could see more clearly how grimy and old the paint in the kitchen was.

When I moved out the whole flat was repainted. I didn't ever see it in its gleaming new creamy glory. Except for the one room that Patrick and I painted.

Needless to say I didn't ever come across a woman who offered to fix the tap. My women friends were all prepared to commiserate about how difficult it is to find a decent plumber, electrician, mechanic, gynae and dentist, and to remind you to hang onto them if you did. But that's the thing about men; they think they can fix things. Or make them better somehow.

Now I live with Paul who knows all about plumbing, rewiring, building, plastering, and painting. He didn't have a chance to try to fix the tap in my flat as I only met him afterwards. He can do things like put roofs on houses. This is not to say he always does the plumbing jobs that need to be done. The gas shower geyser packed up about six months ago, at first he tried to fix it, even bought a new geyser. Then it seems he gave up. Since then there have been other dripping taps and windows that don't close. You know how it is.

# Chasing butterflies

Joburg is unseasonably hot, and Jake is squashed into a small table on the pavement at Nino's in Braamfontein, his favourite lunch spot, just up the hill from Wits. He is meeting his friend, Alice for lunch. Jake wants to persuade Alice that she and her young family should emigrate. He thinks about emigrating every day. He doesn't hold out much hope for the future in this country, this continent. At 70 though, he isn't sure if it matters for him. It's more of an idea of a better life elsewhere, a 'grass is greener' sort of idea. He worries about Alice, and her idealistic husband, Harold, who works for a land claims NGO, almost in the same way that he worries about his own daughter, Emma, who also works for an NGO, a Dutch HIV/AIDS outfit in Kampala. He wishes Emma had decided on a more mainstream life, and he also wishes that she might have found a suitable man to have children with, instead she lives what he sees as a makeshift sort of life, without what he considers a proper home, although he would be the last to convey these thoughts to Emma. He is aware that she probably knows perfectly well what his views are. He hopes that life will be kind to Emma and to Alice, but he isn't optimistic.

Hunched over the *Guardian Weekly*, one of the several foreign papers and magazines he subscribes to, Jake is reading an article about the new pope. How on earth could they have chosen this Ratzinger? He takes it as a personal affront. "What about all those Catholics who will continue to be inhibited to use condoms, even though they're married and have several children?" He mutters, "Married women are the most at risk." He worries about the women at risk from HIV infection, physical abuse; the married ones, the single ones, the old ones. "It's like chasing butterflies, all the things you worry about Jake," Alice says to him one day.

Alice reminds him of his wife, Susan, who died at forty-five. She is earnest and kind, and unaware of the impression she makes on others. She laughs easily and he enjoys her company, she is a breath of fresh air in his life. She is in her late thirties, about the same age as Emma is now. Whatever the reason, he likes her enormously. It is an undemanding friendship. He met Alice in the lift in the building he worked in, when he first moved to Joburg ten years ago. She lived in Yeoville and wasn't married then. Now she consults to the City Council which offers her the flexibility to fetch and carry children. Somehow they started talking the day they first met and within a couple of weeks they were meeting for lunch, picking up on their conversation as though there hadn't been a break. He's listened to her tales of woe about several unsuitable relationships, and more recently through the trials and tribulations of small children, her tricky if tactful mother-in-law, the vagaries of her own mother's mental health as well as innumerable other minor domestic dramas. He usually has some useful counsel for her, or at least a disinterested opinion, which Alice values.

She rushes in, fifteen minutes late, and starts talking before she has even sat down. Every time he sees her she is in the midst of a new crisis. "He made a pass at me, well I think that's what it was. He was squeezing my shoulders, sort of massaging them. Thank God my cell phone rang, I grabbed my bag and didn't even switch my computer off..." She orders a cappuccino and a penne arabiatta, as she tells Jake about her current client's latest outrage. "I mean who does he think he is? It's not as though he doesn't know I'm married, he's had dinner with Harold and me for God's sake. I can't understand him. What on earth was he thinking of? What about his wife? I'm so furious I could punch something. Why does he think he can get away with something like this?"

Before she has finished spilling out her woes, the waitress interrupts them with their order. His is a chicken tramezzino, he eats it all, putting down the triangles in between bites. Jake touches her arm gently before saying, "I would just ignore it, you aren't going to get anywhere taking it up as a grievance. It is awkward though isn't it?" They debate this and other issues while they eat, Jake looking around as though appealing to an imaginary audience, a habit from his days as a university teacher. He flings his hands around as he talks. He is an attractive man at 70, his lithe athletic build makes him look like a long distance runner, but his wiry, white hair gives his age away. The only time he was nearly unfaithful to Susan, comes to mind suddenly. He'd been working late, hoping the Dean would call to let him know if he'd been promoted to Head of Department. He still remembers how his desk looked that night, stacks of books, unmarked exam papers in a teetering pile, the wax crayon drawing of herself as a princess that Emma had done in primary school tacked to his pin board. He'd been staring into middle distance for several minutes. Just as he decided to pack it in for the evening, and was pulling on his coat, Sylvia, one of his grad students, came into his office.

"Please look at my results when you have a chance. There's something I'm not seeing. I need another perspective." Sylvia stood in the door. Beyond her the lab was empty and dark, the others had gone home without him noticing. Both her hands were deep in the pockets of her jeans, as she leaned back against the doorframe, her feet slightly apart, she looked up at him through her thick dark hair. Jake looked past her, like a dog trying to find a way out.

"Uh, sure, let's talk about it tomorrow. I have to dash now."

She smiled, lowering her eyes. "Come and have a quick drink at the Sunnyside, it's on your way."

"No, I can't, not tonight. I'm afraid I have to go now. I'll have a look at your ...um results tomorrow. First thing." He coughed nervously and jingled his keys in his pocket.

"Not even one?"

She was close enough now for him to smell that distinctive musky smell. He sighed, he had been aware of her, this girl, woman, younger than his own daughter, for months now. He had yearned for her, her eager bright mind, her gleaming skin and the hair that he longed to take in his hands and pull towards him, the hair that he longed to bury his face in. Susan was sick for many months before she died.

"No."

"Another time?"

"Hmmm. Yes, another time." He smiled, and reached behind her to switch off the light.

As he drove home that night he thought about the night Emma was born, how he paced up and down that bleak hospital corridor. In those days, fathers weren't expected to be in delivery rooms, in fact they weren't allowed in them. Now you're considered inhuman if God forbid, you don't want to attend the birth of your child. "I was all of 24, we did it all so much earlier then," he thinks. After that everything became more blurry, as though he was on a fairground horse, going round and round, faster and faster. He remembers seeing Emma for the first time, she was so odd and otherworldly, her face a bit squashed, but because she was his, he fell in love with her right away. Susan was tired, her hair damp, but she was smiling as though she'd won a race. She was so full of belief and good will, a bit like Alice.

He thinks of Emma again as he watches Alice finish her cappucino. They always split the bill, he fishes in his pocket for coins for the tip, after peering at the bill for a moment. "I wouldn't worry too much," he pats Alice's back. "If the moment passed, it passed. Just keep out of his way for a bit, especially after dark, or after he's had a lunch meeting, and a couple of glasses of chardonnay," he smiles conspiratorially at her.

Alice swirls her soft tangerine coloured scarf around her neck as she gathers herself together, "You're right. Of course you're right." She kisses him gently on the cheek. "I'm not going back there today, he can stuff off," she calls as she breezes out of Nino's and round the corner. It puts him in mind of trees rustling on an otherwise still day.

# Midnight express

I sat on top of one of the battered old school desks, tired and enervated. The girls were quiet, writing a November exam, I was hardly aware of them, as I stared into middle distance. My mind replayed the events of the previous night.

I'd been sleeping with Carlos on and off for several months. He was Nora's ex-boyfriend. Except that later on they got married, had kids, bought a house, the whole nine yards. Of course at the time how was I to know they would get back together? Our 'dates' followed a pattern, we'd see each other every two or three weeks. We were both 'between relationships'. One of us would phone. He'd always drive to my flat in Yeoville from Norwood, where he shared a house with two earnest young women who worked in NGOs, one of whom had inherited the house from her great aunt. Usually Carlos and I would walk across the park in the dark, laughing all the way to Rockey Street.

We weren't in love, whatever that might mean. Sometimes we'd go to a movie in Rosebank, once we went to a party at Crown Mines and my therapist was there wearing a "Hamba Kahle" David Webster T-shirt. But mostly we'd go to the Midnight Express, and drink. It was usually empty, except for the fish in the large tank opposite where we always sat. He drank Black Labels and I would drink gin and tonics. I'd only recently taken up drinking. I'd been religious as a teenager and in my early twenties. Until I was about 24 I'd never touched a drink. It seemed wonderfully wicked, to be out drinking particularly on a week night. We'd laugh more and more the drunker we got.

I once had to take the morning after pill because we didn't use a condom and it was a time of the month when I could easily have got pregnant. Don't even mention the HIV/AIDS risk.

That night, a Tuesday, we got back to my flat at about two and fell into bed. My bed was a futon on the floor. I didn't have much other furniture in the room, apart from a couple of bookshelves. Most of my stuff was scattered or piled up on the floor. Clothes, shoes, a vase of flowers, my ghetto blaster, bowls caked with dried muesli.

I lit a candle and Carlos climbed on top of me, "I'm a mosquito," he said, whining and wailing and hovering over me, swooping and diving as the noise he made increased.

We laughed and laughed.

"I'm a giraffe," I said, standing up and then bent down to peer at him and nuzzle him and pretended to eat his ears and hair. More laughter. "I'm a rhino," he butted me with his forehead, moving me along as he slowly stomped forward.

"You haven't got a horn," I shrieked. We made our way through llamas, sheep, a canary, a snake, an ant, and many others I can't even remember. At about five, I heard my neighbour flush the loo. The sky had begun to lighten a little.

"Oh shit – I'd better go. Look at the time." Carlos started to dress. There was a strange quiet in the room after all the hilarity. We didn't look at each other. When he was dressed he kissed me gently on the forehead and left.

I looked around at the girls in their blue uniforms writing with great concentration, heads bent, I hoped they hadn't been cheating, I wouldn't have noticed if they were.

# The easier option

One of the big reasons I carried on seeing Louis long past our relationship's sell-by was because I was afraid of his sister. She was a famous activist who'd been in prison for several years; she had a certain angry gravitas that made me nervous. It wasn't the real reason but it sounded convincing to me in weak moments.

It ended badly with Louis. We didn't stay friends afterwards, and we weren't exactly enemies either. If I saw him at the movies or somewhere we would greet each other and have some sort of awkward conversation. At first he didn't want to believe it was over. He kept prolonging things, coming round to my place, acting as if we hadn't broken up, as if there were still things we needed to sort out.

He was so sweet in the beginning, I was a hungry homeless cat, I fell for his warmth.

By the end, we'd fought more than we'd had fun. I was so pathetic I even had to go for polarity massage therapy to help me break up with him. I felt sorry for him, for some mad reason. As though he wouldn't be better off without me; and of course he was. His anger wasn't personal, I see that now, but at the time I was secretly thrilled by how furious he would get. As though his anger was in direct proportion to how much I meant to him.

He didn't have a car when we first got involved. He used to cycle or walk from Brixton where he lived in the garden flat of an influential leftie sociologist and UDF leader. He'd arrive at my flat, his dark curly hair tousled and sweaty. One time we had an arrangement to meet at the Radium, which I completely forgot about. It wasn't like me at all. Later on I was at home after having gone to a movie with Tina, I was drinking a cup of tea in bed, when there was a loud knock on the door. I went to see who it was. It was Louis. I was tempted to pretend I wasn't there, but I let him in. He was sopping wet, his feet were muddy and he looked deranged. He didn't say anything at first. 'You're wet,' I said, stating the obvious.

"I've just walked all the way from the Radium. Where were you?" He was close to shouting.

I suddenly remembered our arrangement. I wasn't sure which way to play it, should I apologise or should I wait for him to remind me and then apologise? I decided on option A. "Oh God, sorry, I completely forgot."

He was strangely cool. "I tried phoning, there was no reply."

"I went to a movie; I've only just got in. I totally forgot."

His wet feet stained the otherwise immaculate parquet, but I felt too guilty to complain. I didn't want him to stay the night in my bed, but it was either that or drive him back to Brixton. Needless to say I took the easier option.

*

I only got really furious with Louis once he had keys to my flat and I discovered he'd taken a bite out of a block of cheese I had in my fridge. I saw his teeth marks and it had to be him, because even though Joseph, the live-in flat cleaner from Tugela Ferry had keys and used them twice a week, he would never have the temerity to open my fridge and bite into a block of cheese. "You're a sad, oversized mouse!" I shouted at him when I saw him the next day. "How dare you?" I didn't have keys to his place, his important sociologist didn't want too many people having keys to the place security threat and all that. So there was no chance of me taking secret bites out of his cheese or anything else as reprisal.

With Louis I constantly felt I was trying to hold boundaries, he was trying to cross them, like an out of hand four year old. I don't know why but the cheese thing really freaked me out. I was scared I would blowtorch him. Even thinking of it now I feel so pissed off and this was what – ten, fifteen years ago?

I used to wonder what Joseph thought of me. He always waved cheerily if I waved first. Otherwise he pretended not to see me, which I didn't mind, it made tricky situations a little easier. I liked him and was grateful to him for his discretion and for the way he made my flat smell of lavender floor polish and Handy Andy and for the clean bath and shiny floors. I liked his deep voice and straight back, his laughter. I often heard him laughing in the street below my flat in the afternoons if I wasn't at work, or from the back of the flats in the evenings.

*

Anyway the first time Louis and I went out together on a 'date' it was to Rumours, in Rockey Street. Every night of the week there was live music there, sometimes I knew the musicians. Jon Voight, that American actor who was in *The Champ* with Faye Dunaway, well he hung out in Yeoville for a while, most people I knew pretended not to recognise him, to give him space and not embarrass him or themselves.

Rumours was a gloomy, smoky place and there were always people to flirt or drink with. It was almost compulsory to go there before you slept with someone. Louis and I drank beer and looked at each other a lot and told anecdotes about our sorry childhoods.

We had a lot in common, same majors at university, he also loved reading and writing and was a good editor. Of all the men I was ever involved with he really liked my family in all their boisterous generosity and madness, they made him feel at home. It was one of the things about him that both warmed me to him and made me suspicious of him. He wore round glasses without frames, they made him a bit geeky, a look I found attractive. He was a little overweight, all the beer, but cute and when he was happy he smiled like a kid.

Before I met Louis he'd been involved with this woman, Arlette, who had two abortions. He was still a little freaked out by this, because he thought she was on the pill. Although he thought he didn't want to be a father, he also didn't want to be the cause of two abortions. He'd been brought up Catholic and it just didn't sit well with him. He insisted on using condoms with me, even though I had a diaphragm. I couldn't take the pill, it made me feel pre-menstrual all the time, bloated, headachy and more than slightly ratty. I was relieved that he used condoms; we were just starting to be aware of HIV/AIDS then. I used my diaphragm and he used condoms, I didn't entirely trust him, not with that track record and he didn't trust me.

In the beginning we were enchanted with each other, he'd come up with these fabulously romantic things to do, like going for walks on the ridge at dusk with a bottle of wine and two glasses. We'd watch the lights come on all over the city, sitting close together, drinking and arousing each other with rubbings and bumpings; intensely more erotic than later on with all our clothes off in bed.

He gave me great presents, a pair of hiking boots, strong expensive ones that lasted for years and before that a pair of black Nike trainers that I wore till they fell apart. I loved the Nikes even though I was a bit dubious about wearing them, the exploited labourers and all. He also often bought me flowers and one year he bought me a dot matrix printer.

I seemed to have enough money to drink Irish coffees and listen to live music, and usually enough to pay the bills, just. Servicing my car was always a financial headache, I didn't understand the meaning of budgeting and it would always come as a huge surprise when I had to fork out R400 for a service and parts. I would borrow money from Louis, or pay on my credit card and then have to stay home at night for a few weeks, till I could afford to go joling again. I never thought about saving, life was too makeshift and uncertain, what exactly would I be saving for? Very few people I knew owned their own places, unless their parents had helped them out or if they had trust funds.

*

Once we went hiking near Pilgrims' Rest, it was utterly romantic. We were happy camping there, cicadas as incessant as the silence in a cathedral. We stopped along the road and swam in farm dams and ate those café-toasted ham and cheese sandwiches on white bread, the kind where the cheese is almost orange and melty.

He introduced me to the palm wine music of SE Rogie, which I loved, and when I hear it now it reminds me of the trip to Swaziland. Rogie's music was very African, but it was an Africa I had only caught glimpses of and wanted to discover more of. Palm wine music is good natured, melodious, and sounds like contagious fun. When we played it on the car tape my spirits would lift immediately, Rogie's flowing deep voice and the light acoustic guitar made me feel as though I was already joling. The world felt bigger, more interesting and more full of adventure.

He told me a story as we were driving that made me see him differently. "I peed in my pants at this border post once, when I crossed into Swaziland in the boot of a stolen car. It was a dark blue Cressida, shit it was hot in there. I had to drive it to Mozambique once we'd crossed over. I was terrified they would open the boot. I don't know if I was more afraid of being found, or of being found having wet my pants." I liked it that he told me the story, for all kinds of reasons. It made me see him as intrepid and vulnerable, a killer combination.

We hiked in pine forests near Pigg's Peak, swam in rock pools at Malalotja, camped there, and drank in bars in Mbabane, just beers, no palm wine to be had. I felt young and beautiful, for the first time in my life sort of in control of things, living the kind of life I wanted to be living. We were cool and relaxed, tourists, but not. I loved the vibrancy of Swaziland, the bright colours and the different energy to that of South Africa at the time. The only sour note was while we were swimming in some rock pools at Malolotja, a squadron of hornets appeared out of nowhere and attacked me and not him. I had to dive into the water to get rid of them. Later when we drove back to Mbabane the stings throbbed and burned, I had an allergic reaction, had to take anti-histamine to bring down the swelling. I felt angry with him, as though he was to blame because he hadn't got stung and because the whole Swaziland trip was his idea.

Several months later I discovered I had bilharzia, more than likely from that trip. I lost weight and had terrible diarrhoea, I don't know why I didn't go to the doctor sooner than I did. So in the end that holiday was somewhat fraught for me and it signalled the beginning of the end with Louis. There was a faulty trip switch that short-circuited the good. We started having small arguments; later on these became full-blown rows, which included him throwing pizza at the walls of my flat. My friends didn't believe me when I told them, he seemed so gentle.

*

By the time it was over between us, we never did romantic things anymore, it was just silence, eating, rows, sleeping in the same bed, our bodies hardly ever touching. I knew that it was also my fault, just being in the same room as him made me feel argumentative and hard done by.

Louis liked drinking; usually he drank beer, mainly Amstels and Castle milk stout, in 750ml bottles, or Guinness if he could get it. In those days you couldn't easily because of sanctions. He also liked buying expensive bottles of Tequila or single malt whisky and drinking most of the bottle in one evening. He frequently had blackouts. He was even sort of proud of them. I think he saw it as living on the edge, risky, even cool somehow. It was a way he could be wild, even though he wasn't wild, not really.

In those last few months, he'd be sunk uncomfortably into the sofa bed in my lounge, pouring glass after glass of Guinness, the sofa bed listing to one side. His dark rage lurked in the Guinness, I was never sure exactly why the drinking unleashed it. I asked Nicky, my therapist, but for the life of me I can't remember what she said. I would sit in the armchair; we'd hardly say anything to each other. I would get up and check on the supper, say chicken curry. He would pick out the raisins and carrots, depending on how much he wanted to irritate me. The built-in two bar heater would only warm a small arc around itself, so I was cold. By then we'd already broken up at least once. I remember wanting to tell him to leave me alone, that it was over for me. But the words would stick to my tongue like flies, and I couldn't spit them out.

I was always hoping he would go home and not sleep at my flat in those last few months. One time I said straight out, "Are you going? I want to go to bed now."

"Well if I'm not wanted," he said, grabbing his canvas rucksack and pulling on his huge grey overcoat. I was too tired to explain, to protest.

I loved having my flat to myself, it felt safe and cocoon-like so much so that I often forgot that people in other flats might be able to see in as I could see into theirs. I forgot to close the curtains when I got undressed at night and would remember with a start. I liked lying on my bed looking up at the blue sky and the plane tree, a view to look into rather than at, a view that allowed me to daydream and drift thoughtlessly as if stoned.

*

When we first started going out he would leave things in my flat. He started by leaving pie packets and empty, plastic-flavoured milk bottles. He would forget to eat and then when he became aware of being hungry he would get me to pull into a garage and he'd buy a steak and kidney pie and a Bar One. Later he progressed to leaving a sweater, his coat, books, a toothbrush, his razor and shaving cream, coffee beans that he would grind to make coffee in the morning.

One time he left half a bottle of red wine that I knew I'd never drink. I hadn't got that clever tip from Nigella yet about freezing wine, even bits from people's glasses, which means you always have handy bits of wine to cook with. He'd leave bottles of Stolichnaya in my freezer. I took to having a couple of shots of vodka most nights, even if he wasn't there.

Louis's anger spilled over and poisoned things. He was one of the men who got onto the carousel with me, circling longer than most, till we were both dizzy and freaked out. We were all trying o find meaning beyond what constituted our lives – work, money, sex, politics, friendship, jols, angst-filled phone calls, daily life.

*

Soon after we broke up, I went to the UK on a work trip, I'd asked my friend, John to take me to the airport. John and I were having a last minute cup of tea, when I heard Louis shout from the street. I looked over the balcony there was his car. "Oh fuck, it's him. I told him you were taking me." I threw the front door key over the balcony and waited. He didn't have a key anymore.

John and I were too submissive to argue. We went to the kitchen to make tea while he sat in the lounge. We tried to avoid eye contact, as we were afraid of bursting into hysterical laughter. We turned on the radio. "I think I'd better go," John said. I nodded.

I sat in the front seat of Louis' white Pulsar, eyes fixed on the view moving by through the windscreen. I was tight and anxious, we'd already driven all over Edenvale looking for a petrol station. He'd insisted on taking me to the airport and then we almost ran out of petrol on the way there. "Typical!" I thought. All the while my inner clock was ticking so loudly I felt my head might explode and my heart burst. Proximity to him brought on this kind of tension.

*I hate you, and when I get back from London in two weeks' time, if I never see you again it won't be too soon. Why did I let you bully me? I would have much preferred to have John drop me off, it would have been fun.*

Light industrial showrooms and billboards whizzed by. I was glad he couldn't read my thoughts.

"So shall I come and fetch you from the airport?"

"No, it's fine, John is already."

"Oh, but," he looked hurt.

"No, really it's too much to ask. You've already had to take this morning off work. I'll see you when I get back. Thanks hey." I pecked him on the cheek, grabbed my bag, "Better go, I might miss my plane." I waved gaily, ignoring the fog of anger and hurt surrounding him. "Bye..." I didn't turn around to see what he was doing and little by little I felt myself relax as I hurried to International Departures.

*

One of the last things we did together was go to Chris Hani's funeral at Els Park cemetery in Boksburg. We went on a hired bus with other people from the Yeoville ANC. There were hardly any white people at the cemetery. We stood at the side of the road and waited for the hearse and cortege to come past. People were toyi-toying and singing freedom songs. Helicopters circled above, there was a heavy police presence. I was afraid that something might go wrong, the police might start shooting.

We got back to Yeoville without incident, feeling heavy with history, we went dancing at Tandoor with a crowd of people and we all got totally pissed. Louis and I eventually stumbled back to my flat at about three in the morning.

*

I lie down, a migraine is crushing me like the teeth of the rubbish truck. I've been brought to my bed, curled up, head pushed into the pillow. The room is dark, I'm in the throes of something, endure it the painkillers lap at the edges, and mercifully begin to unlock ne tension, the thudding recedes to a distant building site rather than right in the room with me. I sleep dreamlessly. Afterwards I always wonder what they are for, migraines, they are like entering a sangoma's cave, where it is dark and it hurts, I'm a supplicant before a jealous god.

I lie on the bed, dreamlessly, for once not thinking about the maze I'm blundering around in, trying to find my way out of. The sheets are cool, the fan whirrs softly. I've unplugged the phone and put the door on the chain. I'm safely alone in the quiet dark, living out these few hours in quiet restorative sleep. When I wake up, I keep my eyes closed and watch myself lying quietly on the bed.

*

Suddenly I never saw Louis around, it was as though he was hibernating or had left town. A space opened up for me where before everything had been closed tightly like the lid on a new jar of mayonnaise.

# THREE POINT TURN

Amanda drives faster than she should down Cavendish Road, she loves the roller coaster ride from the top going down. The lights twinkling faraway to the north cheer her up. She crosses Raleigh Street where it becomes Rockey; the Yeoville streets abandoned to their early morning silence. Only the wind and the birds and a few black women walking to who knows what kinds of jobs are up and about at this time of day. It is Easter Monday, she has left Rupert, her lover of four months, in bed. She decides as she does a three point turn outside the house of Kevin and Max, her friends, "I'm not going back there ever again." She parks as if for a quick getaway.

She thinks of Kevin asleep in his bed, Max asleep in his, this house of gay men, her second home. She has a key, but has never used it this early before. She is too hung over and distraught for her own flat, with its bedroom overlooking the park and lounge overlooking the red-haired woman taxi driver's house and her restless Alsatians. Amanda wants human contact, her flat is too neat, the parquet too shiny, the rooms too empty.

She enters her friends' house from the back, hoping that Max won't be the first one up and about. He is her old friend, from school days in Welkom, a lifetime away. Nevertheless she always feels slightly formal around him, as though she can't forget he was head boy. She makes a cup of tea in the kitchen, everything where it should be in neat, labeled jars. It is more minimalist than her own kitchen, which always has juice, crackers, bread, cheese, tomatoes and gherkins. It's always possible to make a sandwich there, here it's possible only to make a cup of tea.

She takes her tea to the study and switches on the computer, Max is letting her use his PC, hers is in for repairs. The machine whirs and hums as it warms up, her words and sentences appear on the screen. She starts reading where she left off – she's writing a funded report about different possibilities for low cost housing on the East Rand. She sighs, as if greeting boring colleagues at a work function. Oh hello, there you are. She's not in the mood.

Before she has even written a new sentence, she hears footsteps in the passage. "Hi, you're up early," Kevin's face is still soft from sleep, his dusty blonde hair rumpled. He is wearing pale blue and white striped cotton pajamas. No one in her family wore pajamas, it was either t-shirts, tracksuits or assorted levels of nakedness. She's only recently learnt of the joys of crisp cotton pajamas in summer and warm flannel ones in winter from Kevin. Someone better mothered than she was. She can see he is wondering at her presence, she says nothing, isn't sure where to begin or what to say. As though she is trespassing.

"Would you like a cup of coffee? I'm just making."

"Mmm. Yes please. I've just had tea, but coffee would be great."

She restrains herself from following him – the sight of his lanky, boyish, pajama clad body clenches her stomach, fizzes her with anxiety. She waits for the Espresso pot to whistle.

Kevin hands her a cup and sits down heavily in the purple and red kikoi-covered sofa under the window. "Easter's nearly over thank God," he mutters.

Instead of explaining her presence, she says, "Ja, it's such a bleak bloody holiday isn't it? And then the only thing to look forward to is winter. I always forget to go away and then I regret it. You don't want to get on the roads and become a statistic do you?"

She imagines herself sitting next to him on the couch, their legs touching. She wishes she had the courage to stroke him. She knows it would be pointless. Humiliating even. She knows too that if she told him how she felt it would change everything. And not for the better. She wishes he wasn't gay or if he had to be gay that he wasn't only gay, that somehow she could be the woman who would let him see that his sexuality could be less strict, just this once. It probably doesn't work like that though does it? she thinks.

Sometimes she just wants to tell him, so she isn't the only one who knows. She hasn't even told any of her friends about Kevin. She is tired of the endless dissecting of relationships that don't work. She does wonder if Max guesses how she feels, perhaps he and Kevin discuss her light-heartedly, the way she wears her heart on her sleeve. She thinks probably they don't. Anyhow Max lives on a different plane, people and their feelings don't loom large in his inner landscape. She would never talk to Max about Kevin or about anything else that might show her in a vulnerable light, they keep their conversation light, bantering or if they venture into anything serious it would be about some recent outrage in the news or gossip about an official in the department of health. No, it would be too awkward to open up to Max.

She perseveres with the small talk and with drinking coffee. Apart from not having sex , there being no question of sex, Amanda and Kevin have been having an intense affair of sorts. They go for long rambles in the leafy streets of Melrose, Houghton and in the Wilds – something she couldn't do on her own. While they walk they talk and laugh, submerged in an intimacy the likes of which she has never experienced. They talk about what they see, what it reminds them of, they notice things, odd things – like once they saw a woman driving a 4X4 BMW, she was holding the steering wheel with a tissue.

"Maybe it's a stolen car."

"Or I know, she's allergic to leather."

"No, it's her husband, he's a real stickler and he checks the car every night to make sure it's in mint condition."

"Ja, because she's not meant to drive it. It's not her car." They giggle at each improbable suggestion.

They catch buses and minibus taxis all over the place, even to Roodepoort. They take the airport shuttle from the Sandton Sun early one evening to fetch an old friend of his that now lives in London. Kevin teaches her about the joys of public transport. He is from Port Elizabeth originally. More things are possible if you do them with a man, she discovers. She can't picture herself gallivanting around in this way if she was on her own, or with a girlfriend. One Saturday they take the train to Germiston and go to a movie, Lethal Weapon 2, she loves how the audience responds to the baddies being white South Africans. They join in with the audience hoots of laughter at its own jokes. They share the communal delight in the poorly copied accents, and in the identification with being the baddies. In the thawing of the Cold War, East Germans and Russians are no longer suitable villains. Amanda thrills at the sight of Mel Gibson wielding a large semi-automatic weapon as he runs shirtless in the dark, rain glistening on his chest, even though she knows it's completely un-PC of her.

They discover bars on the East Rand and one bar in town, the New Nugget Street Hotel becomes a regular hang out. Christian music plays on the small TV in the corner rather than sports, and the young Portuguese bar tender does his matric Maths homework in between serving drinks. They drink things like Bacardi and Coke, or Klippies and Sprite, trying on different personae.

They go to the Top Star Drive-In and to malls like Southgate. They enjoy the feeling of being visitors, tourists in their own city. She in turn introduces him to the bird hides at Delta Park, the fountains at the rose garden in Emmarentia, Geraldine Gowns in Parkhurst. Kevin particularly loves this shop, it moves him, reminds him of his granny in Port Alfred and the kinds of dresses she wore. He jokes about buying one, a pale blue floral dress with mother of pearl buttons up the front and a soft belt made of the same fabric.

When they drive around in her old dark green Fiat, she plays country and western music about unfulfilled love, nostalgic songs about missing people who have gone off with others. Amanda would like to tell Kevin what he has given her, but she can't find the words, in the end she doesn't say anything, afraid that if she speaks about their excursions, tries to explain what they mean to her, the magic will evaporate.

*

When she finishes her coffee, she asks, "Is Max here?" She knows he is. His car is in the driveway, and his door is shut. Where else would he be? Max's job as an urban planner keeps him working more than ninety hours a week. Either he is at work or at home. His choices leave him little other space especially since he and his long time lover, Josh split up for reasons Amanda still doesn't understand.

"Ja, he is." One of the many things she loves about Kevin is his earnestness, he wouldn't tease her for asking such an obvious question, instead he answers her. He isn't like anyone else she knows, he always speaks kindly to her, never a trace of cynicism. It refreshes her, talking with most other people is a bit like fencing, seeing who can strike first and hardest.

"I've given up on Rupert. It's going nowhere and I've realized I don't even like him. He's so full of shit, pretending to be unavailable half the time. My therapist thinks I need to leave him, practice leaving. Stop waiting for these bastards to leave me. So this is a first. I've officially left him." Kevin nods several times. "Of course I'll still have to deal with him. I suppose he'll phone or something. I'm so sick of these awful men I seem to attract." She laughs a little, "I wish I could find a decent man. Like you."

*

Amanda opens the lounge window slightly. She feels the cool air damp on her cheeks, her long dark hair starting to frizz slightly. A strange chill runs through her as she imagines she hears a little girl calling her, "Mama, mama where are you?" She longs for a child, which is something neither Max nor Kevin knows about her. Time is running out – she wants a baby. She knows she is not going about having one in the right way. She is at a loss.

The last time she had her period, while she lay in bed holding her sheepskin-covered hot water bottle against her belly, and just as the painkillers began to ease the ache, she became aware of wanting to weep. Will I ever have a baby? Sometimes she feels the presence of a child pressing strongly against her. She is already 34, not a spring chicken when it comes to having babies. Her fertility is dropping almost daily, she pictures a barometer, the mercury dropping, one day it will be at zero. Surely I still have time. She has read the research and knows it is possible, but she has also heard anecdotes and knows of several women the same age as her and a little older who want babies and are struggling to conceive in complicated doctor-assisted pregnancies. Others have miscarriages. The very word makes it difficult for her to breathe.

How can I have a baby in this half-baked life I've made for myself? I don't even have a lounge suite, she thinks, let alone a potential father for my baby. She flips through her mental card catalogue of the men she knows. Sweet as they are, none of them are suitable, they all have a Serious Flaw.

Gay.

In a serious relationship.

Serial philanderer.

Drinks too much.

Big commitment issues.

Wrong politics.

Her body is full and fertile right now, but she senses the colder weather of autumn and her barometer dropping steadily. She cradles her belly, I've got to do something differently, or I'm going to miss the boat.

You are gonna be left on the shelf, Amanda. She can hear her mother's voice, her own personal Greek chorus warning her. Didn't I tell you?

But what exactly should I do, Ma? Please St Anthony, help me find a suitable father for my baby. She laughs out loud, now that's a new thought. Listen to what I just said. I'm serious though, St Anthony. You've always come through for me in finding parking spaces, why not a suitable man to have a baby with?

*

Before she leaves for the night she saves her document on a diskette then switches Max's computer off. Max and Kevin are in the kitchen drinking cheap red wine. Music is playing in the background, Abdullah Ibrahim. Newspapers are spread out all over the table. She spent most of the day lying on the couch instead of at the computer reading a book by Mia Couto she found on one of the cluttered bookshelves in the passage. It has been overcast and has rained intermittently for hours. "Ciao!" she calls, "see you soon." They are surprised to see her going.

"Aren't you staying for supper? We've got chicken," Max says.

"No thanks, I must go." She doesn't feel like cooking for them, not tonight. Much as she loves them. She wants to be back in her own flat, eating heated up leftovers, planning her escape. I can't live like this anymore, she thinks as she drives back up Cavendish and into Becker Street. The streets are full now – cars, lights, people, they create a bustle of energy. Music and laughter spill out into the night. I want a baby. More than I want Kevin to want me, I want a baby.

She finds herself talking to her baby telling her things, showing her things. Sometimes while driving she finds tears in her eyes, grieving for a child who should already have been hers. "I've got to hurry," she repeats over and over, in a panicky way, as though she is late for a crucial appointment.

# EATING RABBIT

17th April 1997

Dear Alice

Gavin is driving me mad. I wish we didn't live opposite each other. It was OK when we were involved, in fact nothing could have been more convenient. But now, Ebenezer Street isn't big enough for both of us and not to mention Barb. Seems like she's moved in with him. At first I hoped it was just a fling or something.

She phoned me the other day, it has been decided that we have to Be Friends. Who made up these crazy rules? Not me. But I agreed to have tea with her, more out of – well not idle curiosity, avid curiosity. Will let you know how it goes.

In the meantime things are going well with Martin. We painted the house, an egg-shell white with a bright grass green trim, he knew all about how to prepare the walls, which I've never quite understood before. He whipped up some wonderful blinds out of hand painted fabric from Mali that he bought somewhere in Cape Town when he was there a few weeks ago, and some dowel rods and string.

Back to Gavin and Barbara. The other day they arrived back while I was watering the front garden. Her long dark hair swept around her like a cape and she almost danced into their gate. I wonder sometimes if her performances are only for him, or if she is aware of me watching her too. Some evenings they drum and some of their friends come round, she dances while they drum. Because they do it under the trees at the side of their house, I can see it all. Gavin even suggested that we come along if we like. Doesn't that sound like a Wonderful Idea?

You say you are moving to Greenside? Is everyone deserting dear old Yeoville?

Yours distractedly and obsessively

Tina

*

10th May 1997

Dear Alice

Since I last wrote I had tea with Barb! I would sort of like her if she wasn't involved with Gavin. She's incredibly well-meaning. Although I have to say some animal part of me recoils from her and I'd tear her to pieces, sooner than pass the time of day, so I overcompensated by being kind and interested. She says they are going to get MARRIED SOON! She also said she had been madly jealous and didn't want to live opposite me, but that Gavin had assured her that I was no threat and that I was safely entrenched with Martin. She said that until she met me, she didn't believe him. Am I such a good dissembler? Of course I am a threat, not to her relationship with Gavin, but to her Personal Safety, and yet she doesn't suspect me. Well of course I'm not really, except in thought. Too bad I'm so well brought up, with the old Protestant Work Ethic dyed into my bones, which doesn't even allow me to stretch to bad table manners let alone murder or Grievous Bodily Harm.

Of course I have to keep all of these thoughts to myself. Martin gets bored and irritated with my obsession with Barb. He can't understand it, and I can't either, but I know that even if you don't really understand it, at least you will sympathise.

We've gotten another dog, we're calling him Bruce, after Bruce Willis, though he's got more hair than his namesake. I'm sure he won't be as quirky or demanding as Mojo dearest who has taken to eating tennis balls – at least he's finding a use for them, as he's not a fetcher.

Sometimes he generously fetches a ball, but it always feels as though he is indulging me rather than vice versa.

Oh and by the way, Barbie has now invited me to supper. Well Martin and me. He won't want to go. If he knows what's good for him he will come though. I couldn't do it on my own and of course I have to go. It's too interesting an invitation to let pass. I do wonder why she wants to torture herself? Any ideas?

Speak soon,

Tina

*

May 18th, 1997

Dear Alice

Thanks for your call last night, sorry I couldn't talk for long, we were about to go to a movie at the Monument. 'LA Confidential' was on and movies only show for 2 nights so if there's something you want to see you have to do it at once. I miss that about living in Yeoville, the movies to choose from, the film festivals, live music, Kippies, Tandoor, Rumours. Huge sigh.

I'm doing a writing workshop in PE next weekend, 'Poetry for Beginners'. Been invited by an Arts & Culture sponsored setup. Should be fun – at least it will be some extra cash. Although I love it here, it's hard to make a buck.

The famous supper arrangement is tonight. I'm taking pudding, Martin said that at least there will be something decent to eat then. He's also taken the precaution of buying lamb chops from the fabulous Grahamstown Butchery, in case the food isn't great. He suspects it won't be, given the general flakiness of the cook.

Later, T

*

8th, later on

Dearest Alice

had to write as soon as we got home. Martin is -illing lamb chops. The food was flakey as expected, a chickpea and coriander veggie stew. Barb dished up. I told her I wasn't very hungry as I thought I was coming down with something. I don't know how Martin managed. She gave him quite a big helping. I think he just shoveled it in and swallowed, as though he was at boarding school and the house master was hovering over him.

He was able to have a big helping of Malva pudding, but I couldn't because of "the flu". Lies have to be consistent. Anyway the sight of the gruel, let alone spending more than five minutes in Barb's company made me lose my appetite entirely.

Barbie dressed for the occasion, her hair loose and floaty down to her waist, bangles tinkling, scarves wafting around her like a shimmering halo. You'd think she was specially auditioning for 'aging hippy'.

If that wasn't bad enough, I kept worrying that I might say the Wrong Thing and as a result found it impossible to say anything because I realized I was trying to pretend that Gavin was as good as a stranger, that I barely know him, let alone an intimate shared history, not to mention shared interests and shared friends.
I started to feel quite spaced out by the end of the evening. Gavin and Martin seemed to take the dodgy food and the strangled conversation in their stride. I was relieved you weren't at the supper, because I fear

the tension might have turned into uncontrollable hysterical laughter or something equally mortifying.

Only Barbara battled more than me, she even disappeared to the loo for about 10 minutes. Eventually when Gavin went to see if she was OK, Martin and I planned our getaway, claiming early mornings and important deadlines. Barb looked quite pale when she said goodbye (bulimia?). I thanked her most insincerely for supper. And said we must do it again sometime, where on earth do these scripts come from, they are so deeply ingrained.

Please don't hate me.

Tina

*

June 10th

Dear Alice

I'm so jealous that you've got a documentary film festival to go to, still a few weeks to go before 'The Festival' here. We make do with the video shop's new releases.

Our new puppy, Bruce is a delight, but not like Mojo at all. Mojo tries to make sense of things other dogs don't pay attention to at all. I'm so glad I got him rather than a yappy maltese type dog with a suppurating skin disease and a personality disorder and picky food. Perhaps that dog is still on the cards for me.

Onto the real news, Martin made me promise, in blood practically, never to accept another invitation to a meal at number 63, and I agreed not to. Especially while the present incumbent is ensconced. He put on such a brave face the other night, more of the same would count as torture. I don't think I could bear it either. We'll have to have them back, but I think I might invite a few other people and have a braai, to dilute things a bit. It would be too obvious not to make some reciprocal gesture. It won't be one of those braais where people bring contributions. I shudder to think what Barb might see fit to contribute – a hideous carrot salad set in orange jelly? Or a dish of barley?

Miss you.

Love T

*

June 25th

Dear Alice

It was lovely to speak the other night, thanks for phoning. Festival starts in a couple of days. I wish you'd come down for it. We still have room in our house.

We are going camping at a river near Plett for a week in early September. I haven't been camping for years. Not sure if I'm up to it, but prepared to give it a go. Apparently it's wonderful there. Do you know it?

Jeesh, I've had enough of work, I'm burnt out, feels like a mad enterprise sometimes, working with school principals, stepping in where angels fear to tread and dishing out unwanted advice and suggestions, and generally making a nuisance of myself. Of course everyone is extremely polite, but that's part of it, the formality never really drops off. I don't think I have the stamina for this much longer. It's school holidays now, so no real work for a few weeks.

I lent Barb a couple of books the other day. She said she hadn't read a novel for twenty years, because she Didn't Have The Time!!! I can't imagine what other pressing priorities she had. Apparently she does now. Have the time – that is. Dear old Gavin can't be an all-consuming passionate interest then can he? Well who can be – let's face it.

Barb and Gavin have been in Cape Town at a conference. Gavin gave a paper, and being joined at the hip they went together. It's nice for me though – gave me a bit of a break from her relentless cheerfulness and presence. Sometimes I get the feeling that she is only cheerful to me, underneath all the 'hail fellow well met' stuff there's a sulky 'undertoad'.

According to a reliable informant they plan to be in Joburg, so brace yourself. I'm dying to know what you make of her. If you really like her, I will die, of course. So there you are, no choice but to hate her on sight. Just kidding, I want a totally honest appraisal.

Love Tina

*

July 20th

Dear Alice

Your new house in Greenside sounds gorgeous, double storey and everything. We have come up in the world, haven't we? I love Greenside, such leafy avenues and big gardens, it's wonderful to cycle in. And I hear it's becoming one of the new restaurant & deli districts, which is always handy.

BTW we even have a deli in Grahamstown these days. The lifesaving Italian restaurant opened one in African Street. They sell divine homemade ciabatta, the best I've ever tasted and lots of other yummy things. I must tell Barb about it, in fact take her there and rave about the food, so if she ever plans another dinner party perhaps she could buy in most of her food? Not bloody likely – I think she actually likes the food she produces (I hesitate to say prepares).

Barb has started a trance dance class. I of course won't be joining, but I'd love to be a fly on the wall. Martin says if I'm so interested I should go to at least one class, pretend I'm being an anthropologist. I'm slightly tempted, but I'm too nervous that I won't keep a straight face. Still it won't harm to make enquiries.

The braai I mentioned is tomorrow night, we're having about 10 people over. Will let you know how it goes.

Yours T

*

July 23rd

Dear Alice

Lovely to talk to you, always feels like a stiff sea breeze, refreshing and enlivening.

The braai went swimmingly. Barb outdid herself – she made a cabbage salad – which consisted pretty much only of cabbage. Raw cabbage masquerading as a salad, who would have thought?

We had a fantastically weird incident, which made the whole thing completely worthwhile. A rabbit appeared in our garden, in the part that is fenced off where the pool is, we don't know how it got there, and Mojo suddenly smelt it and started chasing it. He & Bruce barked eagerly while the rabbit threw itself against the fence in a desperate attempt to escape. All of this was a source of great consternation for Barb who kept flinging herself between the dogs and the fenced-off rabbit, wailing and protesting. Martin and I yelled at the dogs somewhat half -heartedly, because we were enjoying the spectacle of Barb playing a form of touch rugby with Mojo and Bruce – the rabbit as ball. When everyone had gone we made evil jokes about rabbit braai. Of course you know me, I'd never dream of braaing a rabbit, let alone eating one, but still it was fun to pretend, if only to give offense. Sometimes I don't recognize myself, perhaps I've turned into my evil twin.

hehehe

T

*

Aug 1st, 1997

Dear Alice

I have to say after speaking to you on the phone last night I felt a bit down. Even just a tiny joke? I thought you would be more anti B. Perhaps she was on her best behaviour?

T

*

August 3rd

Dearest Alice

Thanks so much for cheering me up. I didn't realize that Harry was home when we spoke on the phone. I especially loved that tidbit about B at dinner at Elaine's (I meant to ask – do you still go to Rockey Street?), even though it broke my heart that you guys actually went out to dinner with them. Still I know how it is, social niceties and all that. She is weird though isn't she? To say that at heart she is a gay man? What on earth does she mean? Does that mean that Gavin is a gay man at heart too? Or why would he be with a woman who is a gay man at heart? I wish I could ask Harry what he thought of her. But you know the thing is I'm so avid I think I put people on the defensive. She isn't that bad, they start thinking, I can see it happen. Dearest Harry is so tactful and kind I'm sure he would just mutter something inoffensive.

Barb's asked me to go for a walk, and before I could think of an excuse I'd agreed. I will have to think of several anecdotes and Ten Good Questions so we don't have to have the Heart to Heart that I suspect she wants.

Speak soon

Tina

*

August 26th

Hi Alice

I heard via the grapevine that Barb is thinking of going back to Cape Town. She finds Grahamstown too rough and crass. Still a small frontier town? It's probably just wishful thinking on my part, but please cross your fingers. She didn't say anything about any of this herself, when we went for our walk. I so love Mountain Drive, but I couldn't bear to go there with her, so we walked up near the Botanical Garden. I brought the dogs along, and she eyed them suspiciously. Sadly no rabbits in sight. She spoke about her previous life and told me things about Gavin that I already know.

I have never had such an intense response to someone, and the sooner she's out of my life, my hair, my line of vision, the happier I'll be. I think the thing that really got to me about Gavin and Barb was how conveniently he whisked her out of his hat, like a white rabbit at a magic show. No sooner had I told him about my feelings for Martin and how torn up I was etc, than he had Barb firmly in his life, first in his mailbox and voicemail, and then before you could click your fingers she was living opposite me. I'm going to try and cross-check the grapevine. It's no good asking Gavin outright, it probably won't be the truth, the whole truth and nothing but. All information comes to her who is patient, and if I'm nothing else I am patient and can sit and wait. Like the spider and the fly.

Tina

*

September 20th

Dearest Alice

It's true, its official, Gavin is having a farewell party for Barb! She is going back to Cape Town for a bit. That's the version that Gavin is spinning to save face for all concerned. Apparently she has a great opportunity – doing what exactly? Selling crystals? Teaching trance classes? Whatever and who cares, she is out of here. The party is next Saturday night, and I'm going to go. Martin says he'd rather stay home and watch whatever's on Supersport. I'll let you know what transpires.

WhooooHooo!!

Txx

*

September 28th

Dear Alice

Poor old Barb. I actually felt sorry for her, really sorry for her at her farewell, and for Gavin in a funny way. She danced a lot and the food was divine. I think Gavin must have got other friends to do the catering. They did a ritual with flags and candles in a circle. Gavin played the guitar and sang love songs. Everyone got stoned or drunk. Towards the end of the evening, Gavin built a huge bonfire and Barb danced around it, she was wearing a long gypsy-ish dress , her hair loose and shining. She danced while he played the guitar. I wish I had taken my camera. I felt a bit guilty as though my wishing for her to be gone had something to do with her banishment.

Not that it was spun like that at all. Banishment I mean. It was supposedly only a temporary farewell while Barb went off to do her thing and then she would be back. It was clear though, to all of us that this wasn't a temporary farewell, it was the real deal. This was goodbye.

Txx

Thanks are due to The British Council Crossing Borders Program in 2005/2006 which allowed me to work on the stories with a mentor.

It was a wonderfully restorative experience to be in Kampala at the invitation of Femrite for the writers' residency in 2008 where I finally put these stories together as a collection.

Karen Jennings' sensitive, strong editing enabled me to kill many darlings, even a whole story.

My friend, Colleen Crawford Cousins, has been a true writer's friend in her reading and insight and encouragement.

There are others too, without whom I couldn't have written the stories, but for a range of reasons I don't want to name them. But thank you to you too.

Acknowledgments are due to these publications in which earlier versions of the following stories appeared.

"Plumbing – a short history" in **Kotaz** 3.2 (2002) and in **Half Born Woman** by Colleen Higgs, Hands-On Books (2004)

"Phone you" in **Botsotso** 13 (2004)

"Looking for trouble" in **Dinaane: Short stories by South African Women** ed. Maggie Davey, Telegram Books (2007)

"Spying" in **Green Dragon** 5 (2007)

"Warm enough" in **New Contrast** 37.4 (2009)

"The easier option" in **Big Bridge zine**:
http://www.bigbridge.org/BB14/SA-FCH.HTM

"Chasing Butterflies" in **World of Our Own** and other stories ed. Hilda Twongyeirwe (2011)

# Other titles by Hands-On Books

*Lava Lamp Poems*

by Colleen Higgs

*Difficult to Explain*

edited by Finuala Dowling

*A Lioness at my Heels*

by Robin Winckel-Mellish

*Absent Tongues*

by Kelwyn Sole